LETTERS TO HIS FRIENDS

BY

FORBES ROBINSON

I am your friend

Forbes Robinson

LETTERS TO HIS FRIENDS

BY

FORBES ROBINSON

LATE FELLOW OF CHRIST'S COLLEGE, CAMBRIDGE
AND EXAMINING CHAPLAIN TO THE BISHOP OF SOUTHWELL

EDITED WITH AN INTRODUCTORY NOTICE
BY HIS BROTHER CHARLES

THIRTY-THIRD THOUSAND

9783 849 197 148

PRINTED FOR PRIVATE CIRCULATION BY
SPOTTISWOODE, BALLANTYNE & CO. LTD., LONDON, 1930

NOTE

THIS volume (33,000 copies of which have now been printed) is published privately, and copies will be supplied to any persons who desire them (price 3*s.* 6*d.*, postage 3*d.*, or bound in limp leather with gilt edges 5*s.*, postage 2*d.*) on application to Mrs. C. H. Robinson, 13a *Willow Road, Hampstead, N.W.*3

First Edition, July 1904.   *Reprinted October* 1904,
June 1905, *May* 1906, *October* 1907, *April* 1909,
April 1911, *August* 1913, *August* 1916, *January* 1918,
December 1920, *March* 1924, *August* 1930.

CONTENTS

INTRODUCTORY SKETCH

INTRODUCTORY SKETCH

CHAPTER I

SCHOOLDAYS

FORBES ROBINSON was born on November 13, 1867, in the vicarage of Keynsham, a village in Somerset lying between Bristol and Bath. He was the eleventh child in a family of thirteen, of whom eight were sons and five daughters. His parents were both from the north of Ireland, and his Christian name had been his mother's surname. The motto attached to his father's family crest was ' Non nobis solum sed toti mundo nati.'* Before he was three years old his father moved to Liverpool and became incumbent of St. Augustine's, Everton. He died before Forbes was thirteen, but the memory of his holy life remained as an abiding influence. Thus he writes of him in 1903 :

' The old memories form a kind of sacred history urging me onwards and upwards. I like to feel that I reap the prayers and thanksgivings of my father, that God blesses the son of such a father. The same work, the same God, the same promises, the same hope, the same sure and certain reward. I thank God and take courage.'

---

* Born not for ourselves alone, but for the whole world.

As a boy he was never robust and might even be regarded as delicate. After attending one or two private schools he was entered, at the age of twelve, at Liverpool College, where five of his brothers had been. When his father died in February 1881, the house in Liverpool was given up and Forbes was sent to Rossall. He continued at Rossall till he entered Christ's College, Cambridge, in 1887.

The photograph which is inserted on p. 4 was taken just before he went to Rossall. He was then a shy retiring boy, fonder of reading than of athletic exercise. One who was in the same house with him at Rossall, and who is now vicar of a parish in Lancashire, writes :

'His life at Rossall was not an outwardly eventful one. Not being athletic, he lived rather apart from and above the rest of us in a world of books. The walls of his study used to be almost covered with extracts, largely, I think, from the poets, copied on to scraps of paper and pinned up all round, partly to be learnt by heart and partly, I think, for companionship. He was much older than the rest of us whose years were the same as his. His school life was a time of retirement and preparation for the wider life among men at Cambridge. Though my memory of him as a quiet studious member of the house, more often alone than not, and quite happy to be alone so long as his books were near him, is very distinct, I can recall almost nothing of the nature of incident or about which one can write.'

The present headmaster of Marlborough, who was

also a contemporary at Rossall, writes in a letter to the editor of this memoir:

'Your brother was a great recluse at Rossall, and I much doubt whether you would get any great amount of information about him from Rossallians. I knew him because we were both interested in reading, and I owed a good deal to his influence. . . . You will find, I believe, that his Cambridge days show him in a far clearer light than his school days. I know that when I saw him at Cambridge I realised with pleasure that he was a welcomed visitor in the rooms of very various types of undergraduates, whereas his circle at school had been very limited, and most boys no doubt regarded him as quite "out of it." This is of course to some extent the fault of the athletic standards of our schools, but I also think that he himself developed a great deal socially at Cambridge.'

A sketch of Forbes, by Dr. James, written for 'The Rossallian,' will be found at the close of this chapter. Dr. Tancock, who succeeded Dr. James as headmaster of Rossall a year before Forbes left, writes:

'When I was appointed to Rossall in 1886, I found him a member of the upper sixth form. . . . He always gave me the impression of an earnest-minded, hard-working boy, with a deep sense of duty. It was rather suggested to my mind sometimes, possibly erroneously, that as a younger boy he had felt himself misunderstood, and a certain reserve was the consequence, not perhaps unnaturally. He was already much interested in theological work. . . . It has been a great pleasure to me in later years to hear of his excellent work at Christ's and the strong influence he exerted over undergraduates. It was quite the natural result of the qualities I saw in him at school, provided once his reserve could be broken.'

Though of Irish descent he only once visited Ireland. This was during his summer holidays in 1884, when he travelled round a good part of the north and west coasts. The only adventure of special interest was his unintended voyage across the Bay of Donegal, which was nearly attended with fatal consequences. He and his brother, the editor of this memoir, started in a small open sailing boat from the harbour of Killybegs, intending to return within a few minutes; but no sooner had they got outside the harbour than they were caught in a squall, which rapidly developed into a gale, and made it impossible to turn the boat or head it for the shore, owing to the immediate risk of swamping. The only means of securing momentary safety was to head the boat out into the Atlantic, but as the nearest land in this direction was the coast of America, the prospect was far from cheerful. Eventually the boat was turned a few points further south, in the direction of land which, could not be seen, but which was known to lie about fifteen miles away on the other side of the Bay of Donegal. After having been nearly swamped many times, and running with bare poles, owing to the violence of the gale, the boat arrived at length at Bundoran. As this place was distant some sixty miles from Killybegs,

It seemed wearisome to return by land, and a return by sea was out of the question. Accordingly, Forbes and the writer, drenched to the skin and without a vestige of baggage, started forthwith on a walking tour along the west coast of Ireland, arriving at Connemara in the course of the following week. Forbes's dislike of sea voyages in after years may in part be traced to this experience. During the greater part of the voyage across Donegal Bay he was helpless from sea-sickness; his companion was busily occupied in baling out the water to prevent the boat from sinking.

The letters which Forbes wrote from school to members of his family are a curious mixture of humour and religion. It was his keen sense of humour which preserved him from becoming morbid. It was this same sense of humour which helped to attract to him at the University men on whom he eventually exercised a strong religious influence, but whom religious conversation would have inevitably repelled.

In two letters written to one of his sisters from Rossall in 1886, the following sentences occur. They show that he found time while at school for a considerable amount of reading which was not connected with his school work :

'You ask me to tell you what books I have been reading. Among others, Longfellow's " Hiawatha " and " Evangeline," both exquisite ; continually the " In Memoriam," " Idylls of the King " ; some of Buchanan, which I scarcely recommend ; M. Arnold, which I do most heartily recommend ; and Walt Whitman, the great poet of democracy ; " Confessions of an English Opium Eater," by De Quincey, good in its way ; G. Eliot and Mrs. Browning, &c., &c. Perhaps you would like some of those. I read Chas. Kingsley's " Andromeda "—it is really a splendid rhythmical piece of hexameter—and some of his Life. I rather like pieces of his poetry, and the one you sent me I liked.

' My only birthday advice is : Read more Longfellow. If you have any writers, send me word, though I am sorry to say I can appreciate but few. . . .'

Another letter, written the same year, is entirely composed of selections from Tennyson's ' Princess,' which, he says, ' I have just read through.' He ends, ' Mind you send me gleanings of Milton if you have time.' In another, ' I have been reading a fair amount of Carlyle at present, as we had an essay on " The influence of individuals on great movements of religion, politics, and thought," for which I read especially Carlyle's " Heroes and Hero Worship," and Emerson's " Representative Men," and for which, I am glad to say, I not only got full marks, but the highest maximum possible. Have read Tennyson's " Queen Mary." Am reading " Harold." I liked the first very much, but the latter a great deal more. The scene where Harold debates about telling a lie or the truth is very fine. . . .' The rest of the letter is composed of quotations from ' Harold.' In other letters he says, ' Get Emerson's " Essays " for me.' ' I send you " Aurora Leigh." . . .'

He left Rossall in the summer of 1887, when he

there how great this was ; and it was no little achievement for one whose very modesty and humble-mindedness must have made it difficult. But his heart was in the work, and in the maintaining of Christian influences in university life. It is hard to over-estimate the loss which his death at so early an age implies alike to students of theology and to those among whom he was more immediately working. But he has left us the example of a simple and devoted life and the consecration of great and growing powers to his Master's service. "God buries His workmen, but carries on His work."'

CHAPTER II

LIFE AS AN UNDERGRADUATE AT CAMBRIDGE

FROM this point forward the sketch of Forbes's life can be given almost entirely in the words of those who knew him at Cambridge.

A writer in the Christ's College Magazine for the Lent term 1904 says : ' Many older friends will always think of him in his attic rooms, where he began to make his mark in our College society upon his first coming up. Only two other Freshmen had rooms in College, and Robinson's rooms became at once a centre for his year, and later a meeting-place where the gulfs between higher and lower years were bridged over. A little older than most men of his year, he was considerably their senior in character and in intellect. He showed at once the qualities which he retained to such a unique degree in later years—an inexhaustible power of making friends with all sorts and conditions of men, and an insatiable interest in all sides of College life ; the most serious things were from the first not beyond his comprehension, and the most trivial did not appear to bore him, even when their freshness had worn off. His love of books was catholic ; he possessed a great many and read them

1880.

there how great this was; and it was no little achievement for one whose very modesty and humble-mindedness must have made it difficult. But his heart was in the work, and in the maintaining of Christian influences in university life. It is hard to over-estimate the loss which his death at so early an age implies alike to students of theology and to those among whom he was more immediately working. But he has left us the example of a simple and devoted life and the consecration of great and growing powers to his Master's service. "God buries His workmen, but carries on His work."'

CHAPTER II

LIFE AS AN UNDERGRADUATE AT CAMBRIDGE

FROM this point forward the sketch of Forbes's life can be given almost entirely in the words of those who knew him at Cambridge.

A writer in the Christ's College Magazine for the Lent term 1904 says : ' Many older friends will always think of him in his attic rooms, where he began to make his mark in our College society upon his first coming up. Only two other Freshmen had rooms in College, and Robinson's rooms became at once a centre for his year, and later a meeting-place where the gulfs between higher and lower years were bridged over. A little older than most men of his year, he was considerably their senior in character and in intellect. He showed at once the qualities which he retained to such a unique degree in later years—an inexhaustible power of making friends with all sorts and conditions of men, and an insatiable interest in all sides of College life ; the most serious things were from the first not beyond his comprehension, and the most trivial did not appear to bore him, even when their freshness had worn off. His love of books was catholic ; he possessed a great many and read them

1887.

to his friends. At the College Debate, of which he became secretary and president in his second year, he was a frequent and fluent speaker, with a remarkable command of language, though sometimes his eloquence was more than half burlesque. His powers of thought and real strength in argument were more often displayed in private discussions, where irony and humour hardly veiled the depth of earnestness below.'

During his first three years at Cambridge he read for the Theological Tripos. In the course of his first year he was elected a scholar of his College. At the beginning of his second year he won his first University distinction, the Carus prize for the Greek Testament. The other University prizes which he gained were the Jeremie prize for the Septuagint in 1889, the Burney prize essay in 1891, the Carus prize for Bachelors, the Hulsean prize essay, and the Crosse University Scholarship in 1892. He took his degree in the first class of the Theological Tripos in 1890, and obtained a second class in the Moral Science Tripos of 1891. The year which he spent in reading moral science he afterwards looked back upon as one of the most useful in his life. After he had been reading for some time in view of this Tripos, he wrote to a friend : 'I have come to the conclusion that I know nothing, and am an awful fool into the bargain. . . . The subject is so utterly fresh to me, so completely unlike theology of any sort at Cambridge, that I find it hard to do anything at it. In fact, I chucked it up for about ten days in the middle of the term, and determined to have nothing more to

do with it ; but after that rest I thought better and
renewed the study. It is an excellent training for
the mind. I never distinctly remember thinking at
all before this term.'

Having learnt to *think* himself, his desire was to
help others by teaching them to think. One who
came under his influence several years later says of
him : ' I owe so much to him in every way. Above
everything else he taught me to *think*. I remember
so well the first time I went to him with a difficulty.
I expected him to solve it for me, instead of which,
at the end of half an hour, I still found that I had to
think it out for myself. It was a revelation to me,
and has helped me in my dealings with men.' The
same friend writes : ' I may mention a conversation I
once had with him. He had in front of him the
answers to some Theological Tripos papers. He
took up two of them and compared the answers
given to the same question by the two men. The
answer required was a translation of a passage of
Greek with notes. And, as far as I can remember,
his words were these : " Now, W——, this man has
passed over the real difficulty. As far as I can tell,
he has not even noticed that there is a difficulty. I
have given him two marks out of a possible ten. This
other man has seen the difficulty and grappled with
it. His solution is without doubt incorrect, but that
is quite immaterial. Result, eight marks out of ten."
I cannot but think that this attitude of mind was
largely the secret of his influence.' In another case,
when urging a man to attempt some independent
investigation of the Synoptic problem, he said :

' Your conclusions may be wrong, but you can correct them, and it will teach you to think.'

One who was an undergraduate with Forbes says of him : He ' did not take a prominent part in religious movements in the College, such as the College prayer meeting or Bible readings, though he was occasionally present at them. In chapel his reverence was quiet, though in no way obtrusive. I think that by not identifying himself with any particular religious party he had greater influence with those men whose minds ran in very different grooves. I always felt when in his company that I was conversing with one vastly superior to myself in intellectual powers, and yet he never appeared conscious of it himself. It is surprising how considerate he was of the feelings of others. I remember a large print of Pope Leo XIII. which used to hang in his rooms as an undergraduate, which delighted his gyp, who was a Romanist, but scandalised his Protestant friends. I begged earnestly for a copy of one of his prize essays, which had been printed though not published. He at first consented, but almost immediately asked me to return it, saying that he did not wish it to go out to the world as expressing his matured views. He then asked me to accept instead a small booklet, which he said I should find useful to have in visiting. It contained the verses called " The Old, Old Story." He also gave me a copy of the " Practice of the Presence of God," by Brother Lawrence.'

Before he decided to read for the Moral Science Tripos he had thought of going in for the Semitic Languages Tripos. With this object in view he

commenced the study of Syriac. Finding that the
best Syriac grammar was written in German and had
not been translated, he decided to learn German also.
He was advised that Switzerland was a suitable place
in which to study German, and accordingly, after
taking his degree, he started in the summer of 1890
for Switzerland. The two following letters are inserted in order to illustrate his sense of humour, as
well as to describe the way in which he spent this
summer. He eventually returned from Switzerland,
having made more progress in Syriac than in German,
but without having obtained any great knowledge of
either language. Soon after his return he decided to
commence the study of Moral Science instead of the
Semitic languages.

To H. M. S.

'Habkern : July 1890.

'A few days after I got to Switzerland, by dint of
incessant inquiries and correspondence I found out
the name of a pastor who lived in a sufficiently
healthy place and who talked German. So I girded
up my loins and went to visit him. "Sprechen Sie
Englisch, mein Herr ?" I asked. "Nein" was the reply.
As I scarcely knew a word of German I was in a considerable fix. But I found out that the Pfarrer spoke
"Lateinisch" and could read English a little when it was
written. So I went up to his study and we got paper
and pencil and began. I tried to tell him in a mixture
of broken English and dog-Latin that I intended to
give him the honour of my company. He said he
would be pleased to take me "en pension." He then

asked how much I wished to pay. I hadn't for the life of me an idea of what I ought to pay. " Ut tibi optimum videtur," I said. But he made me fix my price. Then, when I had fixed it, I had to turn it into Swiss money. The good Pfarrer was so pleased with the honour of my company that he took me for less than I asked. Our greatest difficulty next arose : How was my luggage to be conveyed the five miles from the nearest town up a steep hill ? Latin, French, English, German, failed to make me understand the situation. At last I took in the Pfarrer's meaning. I was to send it by the milkman after leaving it at a certain hotel. " Ja," I cried in an ecstasy of joy, at last grasping his meaning, " Ja, ich mittam der Gepäck von der milkman." I arrived the next day. I found the Pfarrer knew Latin, Greek (but he pronounces both quite differently from me), German, French, Russian, Syriac, Hebrew, and a little English. His usual custom is to address me in German. If I fail to understand, he tries Latin and intersperses his remarks with Greek and Hebrew. So my great difficulty is first of all to find out what language he thinks he is speaking in.

 ' Yesterday we were sitting, smoking and drinking, in the village " Wirthshaus " among the natives of the place, the Pfarrer addressing me in Latin, the villagers staring at his learning in adoration and astonishment, and laughing at my attempts at German. The landlord came up to me when I arrived and sent in a bottle of wine for me, refusing to be paid for it, for he said that the natives of Interlaken fleeced the English ; but when Habkern was for once honoured by the presence of one, the people were not going to treat him in the same way.

'It is curious how the Pfarrer goes and sits and drinks and gossips in the "Wirthshaus," even on Sunday, I think. Last Sunday they had a country dance, and very curious and pretty was the scene— the old-fashioned wooden room—the odd national dress of the women—the curiously cut brown clothes of the men—the thick boots—the fiddlers raised above the rest—the quaint urn with its inscriptions above—the gaping crowd of villagers. Then the church is strange—very rude and simple, all white-washed. The women sit on one side, the men on the other. They stand to pray and hear the text, and sit to sing and hear the sermon. The organ and font are placed at one end. The elders stand below the organ, the Pfarrer is lost in the far distance, right up in a big pulpit. The "Predigt" or sermon is every-thing. They have one written prayer before and one after the "Predigt." The people never say "Amen" or anything—only sing. They sing so slowly that, although I had only been with the Pfarrer three days, I could almost sing and look out the words in the dictionary at the same time! I talk German with every one who will talk with me. So well did I spin yarns when I had been in the country three or four days, that with a mixture of Latin and German I managed to make a German use strong language at some of my tales, which he was pleased to think were not exactly true. Reflecting on the situation after-wards, I remembered that I had told him, among other things, that I had walked nearly fifty 'stunden"

In a day. His language was awful. I found afterwards that "stunde" was not, as I had supposed, an English "mile," but an English "hour." But I keep on talking. I have come to the conclusion that the way to learn a language is to argue in it. Accordingly I do so. I have tried to convince them that the order of bishops is semi-apostolic, and that if St. Paul did not actually wear a surplice himself, his successors shortly afterwards did.

'One other thing, if you ever reply to this letter: would you copy out a few of the most thickly marked lines in the "Grammarian's Funeral" in my edition of Browning? They are always in my mind, but I can't quite recollect how they go. There is no poem I like so much as that. I would send you some butterflies, but I daren't kill them. Some of us may have once been butterflies: as M. Arnold says,

'What was before us we know not,
And we know not what shall succeed.'

To H. M. S.

'Habkern: August 1890.

'There is a French pensionnaire staying here, the same as I am. He is very polite, but his tastes are diametrically opposite to mine. He likes wine, walking, women, smoking, painting, violin and piano playing, dogs, and the like.

'He asked me whether I liked the French. I told him "No," and gave him a good many reasons. He abhors the Germans. I told him I thought the Germans were a fine race. I'm occupying my time

C

in sleeping, arguing, observing the natives, and reading a Tauchnitz edition of " Martin Chuzzlewit," which is good, though already a young girl of seventeen has been introduced, very beautiful and all the rest, and I'm afraid she won't be poisoned, but marry a certain young man already introduced. I'd give a good deal to be able to write a novel in which all the young ladies tumbled out of windows, six stories high, and were picked up dead. I think I must try and write one. Shall I dedicate it to you ? The heroine will be a plain old lady with white curls, close on sixty-five, without any money, but with a certain amount of intellect. There will be no marriages, but suicides and murders if necessary.

' I'm inventing a German word of 1,000 letters. It is to be divided into some 150 or 200 compartments. After each compartment there is five minutes for refreshments. After about the 500th letter there will be half an hour allowed for dinner. After the 600th letter or so there will be a notice to the effect that no person with a weak heart may proceed further without consulting a medical man. After about the 980th there will be a notice forbidding any one to go further until their family doctor is in attendance. I have thought of the groundwork of the word—the finished word I'm going to send to M——, as he has the strongest constitution of any one I know. Then I shall get Duke Bismarck to patent it ; after which I shall take out a professorship on the strength of it at Berne. It will, of course, be the " Hauptsache " of my existence.'

Forbes was far from being an athlete, but in 1891, shortly before his ordination, he accomplished the feat of walking with two athletic friends from London to Cambridge in a day, a distance of more than fifty miles. The following description is by Mr. A. N. C. Kittermaster, who was one of his companions.

Walk from London to Cambridge.

Some of us had read that Charles Kingsley had walked from London to Cambridge ; so we determined to follow in his footsteps. We were a party of three—Forbes Robinson, D. D. Robertson, and myself. We spent the previous day at the Naval Exhibition, the night at the Liverpool Street Hotel, and at 4.30 A.M. of Tuesday, August 25, 1891, we started on our fifty-mile trudge. We walked steadily, at first over immense stretches of pavement, till we reached Ware, twenty-one miles out. There we had breakfast or lunch of huge chops at 10.15. After that we took the road again, and did not call a halt of any length till we had put another twenty miles behind us. The day was fine but dull, and we were not troubled by the heat. At the fortieth milestone it began to appear doubtful whether we should all reach the journey's end. I have an entry in my diary : ' At 40 Robertson bad, I worse, Deanlet (*i.e.* Forbes) quite fit.' So at Foulmire, nine miles from Cambridge, we stopped for tea. By this time I was in a state of temporary collapse, but I remember the other two during tea carried on an animated discussion upon the creation as described in Genesis. We all felt better after the

rest and covered the last stage fairly easily, arriving
at Christ's at 9.30 P.M. We had a meal in Forbes's
rooms, fought our battles over again, and retired to
rest about midnight.

The thing which remains with me best is the
amazing ease with which Forbes accomplished the
journey. It is a matter of common experience that
prolonged physical effort reacts on the mind ; conversation becomes difficult, and cheerfulness forced.
I must say that in my case the thought which for a
considerable period occupied my mind was how I
was to get to the end. But it was not so with
Forbes. He travelled lightly, talking happily on all
subjects the whole day. It seemed to make little
difference to him whether he took food or no, and he
was as willing to stop at every place of refreshment
we suggested as to march the whole day without a
meal.

CHAPTER III

WORK AT CAMBRIDGE

IN September 1891 Forbes was ordained as curate
to his brother Armitage, who was at that time vicar
of All Saints', Cambridge. Several of the letters
which are given later refer to his thoughts and feelings at the time of his ordination. His connection
with All Saints' did not last more than a year, as his
brother resigned in the following spring. Forbes had
already been licensed as chaplain to Emmanuel College. He received priest's orders in 1892. In 1895
he was appointed theological lecturer at Christ's College, and in the following year, May 30, 1896, was
elected a fellow. During the same year he was
appointed an examining chaplain to the Bishop of
Southwell.

One who knew him well, soon after the time of
his ordination, writes : ' I cannot remember how we
first became acquainted, beyond the fact that I used
to meet him in the rooms of some prominent members of the College Football XV. All I know is that
several of our year got to know him quite well, and
the friendship grew with time. The fact that he had
distinguished himself in the Moral Science Tripos at

first rather awed me, a freshman. But I soon got over that feeling, for he was the last person in the world to trouble any one with a sense of intellectual inferiority.

'I am sure the private business hours of the Debating Society were some of his happiest moments. His magnificent assumption of wrath on the most absurd grounds; his vast intensity over trivialities; his love for the heat and play of debate, would have made a stranger believe he lived for nothing else.

'Physical strength and virtue seemed to have a strange attraction for him. His assortment of athlete friends was peculiarly wide, and his frank admiration of their qualities gave them a pleasant feeling that in some way he looked up to them—a feeling which I am sure strengthened the hold he had over them.

'He was a tireless walker, and could go far on very little. A party of us used to take long walks, often on a Sunday, to various places in the country. There was generally a volume of Burke or Emerson in his pocket, whose sonorous periods filled the interval when we lunched frugally or rested. I have never known him anything but good-humoured under any conditions. His enthusiasm for our most commonplace jests was unfailing—perhaps one of the surest ways of getting to a man's heart and staying there—and he had a wide tolerance for the minor offences of undergraduate thought and deed. Yet, as for the tone of conversation when he was near, I need scarcely say that one simply did not think of anything unpleasant or vulgar, much less say it.

'I used to admire his immense power of putting

his thoughts into words, but he could be silent too. Sometimes he would come to my rooms when I was working, throw himself into an arm-chair, and absolutely refuse to speak. After a considerable interval perhaps he would consider I had worked long enough, and cocoa and conversation would follow. But it was when I visited him in his own rooms that I remember things most vividly.

' I can still see that little room under the roof ; the picture on the wall of the dead saint floating on the dark water ; the well-filled bookcase ; the table piled with volumes ; himself throwing everything aside to greet one. It was almost with a feeling of awe that I sometimes climbed those stairs and entered into his presence. Perhaps it would be for a lesson on the New Testament—for when I was reading for a Theological Tripos he was generous, even prodigal, of help. The lesson over—and there are many who know what a goodly thing a lesson from him on the New Testament was—he would open a volume of Tennyson—" In Memoriam " most likely—read a few stanzas, and begin to talk about them. Gradually, it would seem, the things of the world would fade from him. He forgot the hour and my presence as his thoughts poured out. I sat and listened, generally silent, sometimes hazarding a question. Presently— it was often late—I would rise to leave. Rapt from his surroundings, he seemed scarcely conscious of my departure ; and I would go quietly out, almost as though I had been on holy ground, where not once nor twice the dweller had seen God face to face.'

His power of helping men by silent sympathy is

referred to by one who writes : 'The many words of kindness, but more particularly the silent sympathy he conveyed in some mysterious manner, will ever keep him present with us.'

Another, who had known him in his early days at Christ's, and again in later years, writes : 'When I was up he was a nervous retiring man, at his best when one found him alone in his own room. Even then he would sometimes talk little. Since my return from South Africa I have found him much more at home with men and much more ready to talk, but retaining his old power of sympathy without words.' His own faith was based rather upon intuitive perception of the Divine love than upon argument. On one occasion, quite towards the end of his life, he said to one with whom he was staying, ' Sometimes I sit and think, till I can find no reason for the existence of God ; and then there rises up in me something which is stronger than the love I have for those who are dear to me—and they are very dear—the love of God. It seems to smile at my doubts.'

Several of his friends have referred to Forbes's influence as a power which helped to develop their own sympathy towards others. Thus one writes :

' I think perhaps it was my intercourse with him that first taught me to look out for and appreciate the real goodness—or, better, Christlikeness—of others from whom one differed in important matters and with whom one seemed perhaps to have little in common.'

In some instances friendship between Forbes and an acquaintance seems to have arisen where very little direct intercourse had taken place. One who was greatly his senior says of him, 'I have never known any one with whom there was so strong a sense of intimacy founded on so little positive intercourse.'

In July 1892—*i.e.* about nine months after his ordination as deacon—he took part in a kind of peregrinating mission tour through part of South Cornwall. Dressed simply in cassock and cape, and carrying a small brown paper parcel containing necessary luggage, he and his brother (the compiler of this book) walked from village to village, preaching afternoon and evening in the open air. At the end of the evening service an appeal was made to the people. It was explained to them that the preachers had come without provision or money, and hoped to receive hospitality from those to whom they ministered. Night after night Forbes and his companion were taken in and entertained, often by very poor people. A unique opportunity was thus afforded of getting to know something of the home life as well as of the religious beliefs of the poor. As a rule, those who acted as hosts were Nonconformists. Forbes spoke once or twice each day to the people who gathered, and his addresses, which were generally based on the words 'Our Father,' were admirably suited to the comprehension and needs of the simple country people.

For several months during 1895 he took charge of a small country parish near Cambridge, called Toft. While staying at Toft he wrote to a friend, 'I like living among country folk and talking with and visiting them. I want to get out of my life into their lives. This parish work humiliates if it does not humble one. . . . The smallest parish is a tremendous responsibility.'

The following are a few additional notes contributed by others who knew Forbes at Christ's : 'His broad sympathies, his unfailing efforts to find out the good in persons and systems—the rays of truth which each possessed—combined with the rare faculty of going deep down beneath vexed questions, and thus lifting controversies to a higher and serener atmosphere : these were qualities in him which were known especially by those privileged to have more intimate knowledge of him than that vouchsafed by formal lectures or social gatherings. . . . He is now another link with the life beyond these conflicting voices, one "who loved Heaven's silence more than fame."'

The same writer says of him in another letter : His extreme fairness and toleration, which at first seemed to me to reduce half one's cherished beliefs to open questions, was of the greatest value in dispelling ignorance and prejudice, and in promoting true charity and a more intelligent faith. He delighted to call attention to the fact that our Lord found something commendable and exemplary in the serpent. And so, in dealing with those with whom he most disagreed, he tried to fix attention on that portion of truth which lay behind their opinions, or on those real difficulties, to be slighted only by the superficial, with which they were grappling. Tertullian, with his love of scoring off opponents, fared badly at his hands, and he used to treat Clement of Alexandria more sympathetically than Irenæus.

' It was striking to find a mind so evenly balanced and philosophical become fired with enthusiasm as he spoke in simplest language, in chapel or elsewhere, of great Christian truths or the victories of faith. His sermons influenced, I believe, many of the naturally careless. Simple, impartial, earnest and sympathetic, he won, I know, the deepest affection and respect of many.'

Another writes : ' Bright, pure, and strong—this was the impression he gave me . . . . Many men will be very sorry that he is not here any more, but every one who *knew* him will be very thankful that he *was* here, and that they had an opportunity of hearing him "think" sometimes. I recall him most in his own rooms, beginning to talk on some small matter, and gradually lifting us higher and still higher, until we all silently listened, following as best we, with our muddier minds, could ; and even when he got beyond us there were still inspiration and strength to be got from his flashing eyes and on-rushing earnestness ; but if some smaller mind broke in, in a moment he was down at the level of that mind, half bantering and wholly sympathising. Nevertheless, some of us have never forgotten the things he showed us as he led us up, and the possibility of soaring very high without losing touch with those whose levels are pathetically human . . . . I do know that he helped me much, and that many things he said I shall never forget, and thank God for still.'

A Cambridge and international athlete, an intimate friend of Forbes, writes : ' Though I have lost your brother Forbes, and life will be for ever poorer to me, I can't thank God enough that I ever knew him and loved him, and that he called himself my friend. He was so dear to me—my greatest friend in the world. His goodness and his help to me in my Cambridge days were wonderful. He altered my life. God has called him home and to the blessed rest of the children of God, and we are rich still with his memory and the influence of his beautiful, patient, Christlike life.'

In another letter he writes : ' The death, or, as I like to think of it, the passing of Forbes into the Great Beyond has been such a grief to me. You have no idea what he was to me—a real man " sent from God " into my life. I could do nothing when I heard the sad, and to me utterly unexpected, news, but kneel down by my bedside, and weep till I could weep no more for my beloved friend. I feel so rich and proud to have had him for my friend, and to have had his love ; and so do many Cambridge men. Oh, but I did so love him ! and my prayer now is that the memory of him with me always may strengthen my weak and feeble life, and help me to live somewhat more as he lived, very near the Master.'

He obtained but little help from self-introspection or self-examination. Thus he writes in one of the letters given later on : ' I am not sure that we cannot learn more about others than we can about ourselves.

I never think it is profitable to study oneself too closely. I never could meditate with any profit on my sins. But there, I dare say I differ from many others.'

To very intimate friends he would in rare instances admit that the secret of any influence which he possessed over men was the outcome of his efforts to pray for them. One who had known him intimately at Christ's writes in 1904 :

'About eighteen months ago I had the privilege of spending a night with him, and then for the first time I realised how much of his spiritual power was the outcome of prayer. He told me that in his younger days he had taken every opportunity of personally appealing to men to come to Christ. " But," he went on, " as I grow older I become more diffident, and now often, when I desire to see the Truth come home to any man, I say to myself, ' If I have him here he will spend half an hour with me. Instead, I will spend that half-hour in prayer for him.' " Later on, when I had retired for the night, he came to me again and said, " W——, what I have said to you is in the strictest confidence : don't mention it to any one." And this revelation of his inner life is my last memory of him.'

On another occasion he said to one with whom he was staying, when speaking of the little that men could do for each other, ' I think that I should go mad were it not for prayer.'

As an instance of his common sense in a matter in which as a bachelor he could have had no personal experience, he strongly urged a married man, before

deciding to accept a curacy which had been offered
to him, to let his wife see the vicar's wife or women-
folk. 'She will know intuitively,' he said, ' whether
she can get on with them and they with her, and it
will make all the difference to your work and happiness.' The man to whom this advice was offered
writes : ' The advice was given seriously, but with that
bright twinkle of his ; and I owe much to it, for we
have been here since . . . and I don't want to go.'

The following is an extract from a notice which
appeared in the ' Guardian ':

' By his published work he is best known to the
outer world as one of the few English scholars who
have given attention to Coptic. In 1896 he edited
" The Coptic Apocryphal Gospels " in the " Cambridge Texts and Studies." The important article on
the Coptic Version in Hastings's " Bible Dictionary "
came also from his pen, and he was engaged on an
edition of the Sahidic fragments of St. Luke's Gospel.
His deepest interest, however, lay not in these sub-
sidiary studies, but in the fundamental problems of
theology proper. His Burney Prize essay, printed at
the University Press in 1893 under the title of " The
Self-limitation of the Word of God as manifested in
the Incarnation," is no doubt comparatively slight,
and in some respects immature ; but its reverent and
fearless treatment of the difficulties of his great theme
gave promise of work of permanent value in this field.
His interest in the great problems never flagged, and
his sympathetic touch with the life and thought of
the younger men in his college kept him constantly

engaged on the task of putting into clear and ever
clearer expression such solutions as he was able to
attain. His sermons in College Chapel were singularly effective, because he never wasted a word, and
because every sentence was felt to be the outcome of
strenuous thought tested by living experience.

' It is not surprising, therefore, that he exercised
an unusual influence upon younger students. His
friends were very closely bound to him indeed, in
bonds which death can consecrate but cannot sever.
They can never cease to thank God for the pure,
bright, tender, utterly sincere, fearless, and faithful
spirit He has given them to love.'

CHAPTER IV

THE LAST FEW MONTHS

FROM the time that Forbes took his degree at Cambridge his health was far from strong. He suffered from time to time from a form of eczema which caused him a good deal of discomfort and pain. Many of his letters contain references to the fact that he had been unwell and had been unable to do as much work as he had hoped. In September 1897 he went with his brother Armitage on a visit to St. Petersburg and Moscow. He stayed in the house of a Russian priest at St. Petersburg, and was much interested in the work of Father John of Kronstadt, with whom an interview was arranged which unfortunately fell through at the last moment. Towards the end of 1897 he developed a bad cough and was threatened with phthisis. He accordingly spent Christmas and the first two or three months of 1898 at St. Moritz in Switzerland. His health then seemed to be much improved. For several years he went back to St. Moritz to spend the greater part of the Christmas vacation. He took great delight in tobogganing, and on one occasion was awarded a prize for a race in which he took part. In the summer of 1899 he went out to South Africa

during the Long Vacation. He visited Pretoria and
had an interview with President Kruger and his wife.
One of his letters records his impressions of the President. He was for some time disposed to believe
that the war, which broke out soon after his return,
could and should have been avoided, but he subse-
quently modified his views on this point.

Towards the end of August 1903 the pain from
which he had suffered intermittently for years became
so much worse that he came up to consult a London
doctor, and by his advice remained in town as a patient
at St. Thomas's Home. When he entered the home
he fully expected to undergo an operation within
a fortnight ; but the doctor who had suggested it
declared, after further examination, that no operation
was necessary. Meanwhile Forbes lingered on in the
home week after week. Eventually a partial operation was performed, and after he had spent thirteen weeks in the home the surgeon suggested his
removal to a private nursing home, where he could keep
him under closer observation. Here he performed a
second operation. This seemed at first to have been
a success, and after a fortnight in this private home
he was well enough to start for Switzerland again.
He went at first to St. Moritz, where he had been so
often before ; but, finding that the pain returned and
that he could not sleep, he went down to Alassio on
the Riviera. Here he was for several weeks till his
return to England. He reached Westminster on
January 13 and went up to Cambridge on the following day. For a few days he was well enough to
lecture, and it seemed as though he might be able to

resume his old work. On Sunday evening, January 17, he was 'at home' in his rooms and received over sixty undergraduates who came to welcome him back. Soon the old trouble returned, and he rapidly grew worse. His pain became almost constant, and he was removed with great difficulty to another London nursing home on January 29. It was then proposed that the original operation which had been suggested, but had never been performed, should take place, and he fully expected that this would result in his restoration to health and to work. A few days later he was threatened with blood-poisoning, and it became obvious that the operation must be delayed. On Saturday evening, February 6, he seemed fairly cheerful. Neither he nor his doctors had any idea that he was in an extremely critical state. About midnight, as the pain had become worse, his doctor was sent for, and he gave him an injection of morphia. Soon after this he asked his nurse to turn the light down and said to her, 'If I am asleep in the morning do not wake me.' She looked in about 3.30 A.M. to see if he was asleep, and, finding him awake, inquired if he would like a drink of champagne. He said yes, and asked her first of all to help him turn over to the other side. As she was in the act of assisting him, he passed away, without a movement of any kind. A happy smile lingered long on his face after the end had come.

His body was removed the same evening to St. Faith's Chapel, in Westminster Abbey. Here on the following Thursday morning, February 11, at 9 A.M., the funeral service was said. The chapel was filled with his friends, who had come from Cambridge and elsewhere. His body was buried the same afternoon at Eastbourne in the same grave with that of his sister, the Deaconess Cecilia, who had passed away five months before.

The inscription on the memorial card issued to his friends was:

CUM CHRISTO VICTURUS
DE MORTE AD VITAM MIGRAVIT
DOMINICA IN SEXAGESIMA
ANNO SALUTIS MCMIV
ÆTATIS SUÆ XXXVII.

And, doubtless, unto thee is given
A life that bears immortal fruit
In those great offices that suit
The full-grown energies of heaven.

CHAPTER V

TWO APPRECIATIONS

THE two following sketches of Forbes Robinson's life at Cambridge have been contributed, the first by the Rev. T. C. Fitzpatrick, Fellow and Dean of Christ's College, and the second by the Rev. Digby B. Kittermaster, of Clare College, now Head of the Shrewsbury School Mission in Liverpool.

Mr. Fitzpatrick writes:

'College life has changed a good deal since the days when a young graduate, on his election to a fellowship, was advised not to see too much of the undergraduate members of the College, that the division between the senior and junior members of the College might be preserved. A custom of that kind, once established, is not easy to break, for traditions of all sorts, good and bad, live long in College.

'Fortunately, the relations between the under-graduates and the fellows of the College are gradually becoming more natural, to the benefit of the whole body. Forbes Robinson will be long re-membered for the influence that he exerted in this direction, and what he has effected it will be comparatively easy for others to carry on.

'It is my desire to give some slight impression of his life in College, and I do not wish to say much about his teaching work. I must mention, however, what frequently struck me, the great joy he had in teaching ; his success was not surprising. When he found (in January last) that he could not take up all his lecture work he would not allow another to give in his place the course of lectures on Church History. " I want," he said to me, " to give them myself in my own way," and he hoped to have given them this Easter term. I was not surprised to hear from a pupil of the interest that he and others found in a similar course of lectures which he had given the previous year. " He put things so," the pupil told me, " that you could not forget what he had said."

'My last recollection of him as a teacher bears witness to his interest and purpose. Word was brought me before morning chapel that he had been obliged to call in the doctor in the middle of the night. I went to his rooms after chapel and found that he was asleep. I put up a notice that he would be unable to lecture. He awoke soon after I had left his rooms ; he had another notice put up that he would lecture in his rooms. When I came back to College later in the morning I looked in and found him lying on his sofa with the room full of men, sitting where they could. The class will not forget that lecture, nor shall I forget the sight.

'When two men have lived a number of years within the same College, it is difficult for them to

realise the change in their relationship that has come
with time. There is a comradeship that comes
through the influence of circumstances rather than
from that personal attraction which two men feel for
one another, and which arose they don't remember
when or how. It was this comradeship of work and
the sharing of responsibilities that led me to know
Forbes Robinson. We had lived some years in
College before I knew much of him ; I was some
years his senior, and our lines of work were very
different. As far as I know, he never talked to older
men in that frank way which was his custom with
those of his own age, and still more with men
younger than himself. Some weeks ago I was staying at the hotel on the Riviera where he had been at
Christmas time. The English lady, whose husband
keeps the house, told me that with them Forbes
Robinson hardly talked at all, but that he took their
boy out for long walks and talked to him ; and the
boy's face lit up as I spoke to him of Forbes.

'There is still the recollection in College, handed
on from year to year, of the walk which he took at
the end of a Long Vacation from London to Cambridge with two other men, and how he talked all the
way. It was these conversations, often prolonged
for two or three hours, that impressed those to whom
he opened out his thoughts, and who in turn let him
see something of their inner life.

'Forbes always had one or two special friends
among the younger men, whom he seemed to me
to look upon as heroes ; he always yearned for sympathy, and he was prepared to give to others all that

he had got. This closer relationship with a few men did not in the least narrow his interest in the life of the College. He gained, I cannot believe that it can have been without an effort long and hard, the power of taking an interest in all sorts of things that form no small part of the life of the average man. There was nothing strained or exaggerated in his relations with other men ; he was at all times just himself.

'When he was elected a Fellow, being also Theological Lecturer, he was anxious to do something to interest and help those who were not theological students, and he had, first on Sunday mornings after Chapel, and afterwards in the latter part of the afternoons, Greek Testament readings for non-theological men, and some terms he took up some of the problems that present themselves as difficulties to the thoughtful man. These papers were prepared with great care, and, as I know, at no small cost of time and energy.

'On Sunday evenings he was "at home" from 9 to 11 to any members of the College who cared to come. On those occasions it was a curious sight that met the eyes of any late comer as he opened the door and saw men in groups sitting on the floor, as chairs were insufficient ; as a rule there was no general subject of conversation—numbers made that impossible. Most Sunday evenings there was music, but not always, and it was difficult at the end of the evening to say what could have brought so many men together. It was a common ground of meeting for different kinds of men. Forbes Robinson was often at his best on these occasions ; he would join

first one group and then another, and take part in the
subject which was being discussed. Generally one or
two would remain when the others left, and deeper
problems would then be talked over. Only on one
Sunday of last term was Forbes Robinson well enough
to be " at home." The room was more crowded than
I had ever seen it. It was a sort of welcome back
after his absence the previous term. It was evident
that it gave him pleasure, and evident, too, that he
was all the time in pain. Yet with a brightness,
which must have cost him much, he talked with
one and another of simple daily interests in the way
that showed his sympathy with life, and gained for
him the power of saying on other occasions deeper
things.

'Nothing could have been simpler than the character of these gatherings. Simplicity was the secret
of his power.

'I find it impossible to write of my own conversations with him; they dealt chiefly with the
difficulties of Cambridge, of College life, and of the
lives of those in our College for whom we felt we had
a responsibility. Talking of the difficulties of belief,
I was struck by his quiet answer: " I do not believe
some things which I did when I was younger ; but
those which I believe, I believe more firmly." Forbes
Robinson had a great belief in the power of intercession. Quite recently a man in his year told me
that when Forbes Robinson was an undergraduate
he had known him spend two hours during the afternoon in intercession for his friends. One is not
surprised that prayer was a subject on which he

thought much. He was to have written an important article on it.

'As we talked together of different men, I remember being struck with the desire he expressed that men should be good and strong, and not of any one type. He had a great confidence in the essential goodness that there is in men, and he always formed a high estimate of another.

'His letters will indicate how deeply he entered into the lives of others, and how wide were his sympathies. A member of another College told me that the news of the death of Forbes Robinson reached him just after the close of their evening chapel, and he had not long returned to his rooms when an Indian gentleman called, an undergraduate of this College, who almost in tears told him of all that Forbes had done for him, and how he had learnt in Hall at Christ's from the strange silence that something must have happened, and was told of the loss that came so unexpectedly upon us on Sunday, February 7.

'I close this short account of my friend with extracts from three letters casually taken from those which have reached me. A young clergyman writes : " I feel I owe a very great debt to him, both as a lecturer and as a friend. His clearness of mind and power of thought were such as I have never seen in any other man. But far more precious than these intellectual gifts was the inspiration of his personal character. His ideals were so high, and he lived so close to them. Few lives have better expressed the truth of the words of which he was so fond : ' He that

loseth his life shall find it.'" A schoolmaster writes:
"The last talk I had with him was a month before
my ordination, and I remember the emphasis that
he laid on the praying side of a clergyman's life."
A doctor writes: "Looking back upon my time at
Christ's, I think that of all the influences which
helped me, the most potent was my friendship with
Forbes Robinson. . . . I came to know him somewhat intimately by spending an Easter vacation with
him, and several of our conversations then have left
a lasting impression on my mind. . . . I suppose, as
one gets older and sees so much more of death, that
a deepening faith takes away that sense of personal
loss and leaves behind a feeling of gladness that yet
another friend has passed to the Communion of
Saints."

'Of his life we may use the motto of his College:

'AD HONOREM CHRISTI JESU ET FIDEI EJUS
INCREMENTUM.'

Mr. Kittermaster writes:

'Forbes Robinson did not regard any one of us as
a "mere undergraduate," one of a mass; that was the
first thing which those of us who knew him as undergraduates learnt. He was genuinely interested from
the first in his undergraduate acquaintances; interested in them as men, not as promising pupils, not
as likely scholars, not as athletes, not as material
for "improving" influence, but as men—individuals,
each possessing a separate and distinct human per-

sonality, and therefore of the truest and deepest interest to him.

'Our public schools taught us (and for most of us Cambridge continued the teaching) that to be of any real importance and consequence among his fellows a man must be "good at games," or perhaps— but this more rarely—"good at work." Such is the simple creed of the undergraduate. If he satisfies neither of the above requirements, then he recognises, with greater or less sadness, that he is an ordinary man, the "average undergraduate." He is one of the crowd if he has no athletic powers to commend him to the notice of his fellows *in statu pupillari*; he is one of the crowd if he has no slightest hope of making for himself any name in the intellectual world, to commend him to the leaders of thought at Cambridge. And this knowledge is to many a Cambridge boy, playing at being a man, a matter of real, if unconfessed, grief.

'But "there is no such thing as the average man, or at least as the average undergraduate." This was the belief which Forbes Robinson held with increasing conviction as his life went on. And it was this belief which accounted to some extent for the very large part which his friendship undoubtedly played in the life of many a Cambridge undergraduate.

'For a man condemned by his fellows and himself to the position of the "ordinary man" found himself in the presence of Forbes (as all of us universally called him) to be no such thing. Gradually and with genuine surprise he learned from him—not by any definite word of teaching—that though it might cost him efforts painful and many to get the better of his "special," and though athletic fame knew him not at all, yet the possibilities of his own peculiar personal life were wonderful and great. For here was one who compelled men by his genuine unaffected interest in their lives and work to be themselves genuinely interested in them too. A man could not know Forbes for long and not be quickly conscious of a new sense of the value of himself, which made him believe that his own personality and life were things of great importance. For "He is interested in me" is what almost every man felt from the start of his acquaintance with Forbes. "He is interested in me" we felt when he passed us in the street with his quaint humorous smile of recognition; we felt the same when we entered his room, to be received often without a word but with the same half smile: we felt the same again if we knew that he was watching the progress of a football match or boat race in which we were taking part. And "he is interested in me"—most wonderful of all—we felt as we listened to him in the lecture room, and were compelled to attention; for his interest in the men in front of him, coupled with his interest in his subject, forced us all—pass men and honours men alike—to listen to the history of Church and Doctrine and Creeds. It was this unfeigned interest in men, simply as men, that in the first instance gave him the influence which he certainly exercised over all sorts of men, including the kind of men whom the majority of their fellows disregarded, or perhaps despised ; " the babes and sucklings of the undergraduate world," to quote another. Such men, in whom most of us could find little to attract us, were to him vastly interesting—interesting for their simple human personality.

'Some men perhaps never discovered from what source his interest in them sprang. They knew that their views of the possibilities of their own life were enlarged, that they believed in themselves more for having been with him ; but it was not all at once that they discovered the reason of his interest and belief in them. It was due to the Christ. With each new friendship and acquaintance which Forbes made —and this is especially true of young men—he saw deeper into the meaning of the Incarnation of Christ. This was the secret of his extraordinary interest and amazing belief in nearly every one of us. He saw in us all, however ordinary, however commonplace— yes, however unlovely were our lives—something somewhere of Jesus Christ.

'Then some of us were privileged to discover that what he felt for us was something far deeper and holier than is expressed by the word "interest." It was love. In every fullest sense he understood the grand full meaning of the word. His love for his friends was something altogether larger and deeper and truer than is generally understood by the word. It was so holy a thing that it is hard to write of it. He knew, and the knowledge is perhaps rarer than is supposed, what in all its fulness was the meaning of the love of one man for another. This is why he could enter into the spirit of Tennyson's " In

Memoriam" as almost no one else could. Tennyson's experience might have been so entirely his
own. His love for his friends was indeed a wonderful, sacred thing, beautiful to see. With Henry
Drummond he felt that it was better not to live than
not to love. Love was to him a part of all his being:
for in him dwelt "the strong Son of God, Immortal
Love," compelling him to love his fellow-men.

   ' It was to him a real grief that (as he often quite
wrongly supposed) one or two of those, for whom he
would quite willingly have cut off his right hand if
in any way it could have advantaged them, cared
not at all for him, nor ever understood how he cared
for them. But he found relief from the strange unsatisfied longing, engendered in him by this belief, in
intense continuous prayer for those whom he loved.
He prayed, it is certain, as few men pray. Prayer
was to him the very breath of life. And his prayers,
like his life, must have been utterly selfless. Many
do not understand the amount they owe to his
prayers. Some of us may some day realise the
magnitude of the debt; at present it is not seen.
But he prayed with all the effort of his being for his
friends : eagerly, passionately, unceasingly he prayed.
"Pray for him, believe in him ; believe in him, pray
for him," he was never tired of saying to those who
spoke to him of some disappointing friend. And his
own life was a proof of the power which lay behind
such prayer.

   ' To those reading this who did not know Forbes
Robinson it may seem that a man of such intensity
of feeling and holiness of life would be more likely

to frighten away than to attract to close quarters the " average undergraduate " (whose existence he denied). This most certainly was not the case. For, if there was in him something utterly divine, he was also human as ever man could be. He admired, like the veriest freshman, the physical strength and powers of the athlete. In his presence the man of bodily attainments and strength of limb experienced the strange sensation of being looked up to by one whom he knew to be utterly superior to him. But perhaps nearly all who knew him experienced this at one time or another; for he must have been one of the most humble men that have ever lived. His humility was almost a fault. It led him to depreciate himself so far. And yet how beautiful a thing it was! He did indeed count all men better than himself.

' He easily condoned offences which in some eyes, and especially the eyes of dons, loom as a general rule heinous and large. And the riotous under-graduate, who cuts chapels and lectures, found that a don—yes, and a junior dean—could be a friend of his.

' He possessed too a keen and real sense of humour. He could, and often did, laugh with all his heart. He chaffed continuously his large circle of undergraduate friends. When he was questioning a man in the lecture-room, you felt that all the time he was half chaffing him. He addressed us all in lectures as " Mr.," in a half serious, half amused style. " It is the only chance for some men to retain any self-respect—to address them as ' Mr.' "—he would say, after the discovery of some more than usual piece of ignorance in his class of "special" men ; "for how can a man have any self-respect unless addressed as 'Mr.' who does not know which are the Pastoral Epistles, or who is the Bishop of Durham (then Bishop Westcott) ?"

'He could not remember the name of his best friend on occasions, and he would recount with real glee how he had been known successfully to intro- duce two men, not knowing the name of either. On one occasion it fell to him to introduce to each other a low-caste West African native and a particularly high-caste Brahmin rejoicing in a lofty sounding polysyllabic title : of course he transposed the names —with results, so he declared, almost fatal to himself.

'He would display with humorous pride to his athletic friends a photograph of himself coming in second in a toboggan handicap race at St. Moritz, which he always maintained he morally won. He was full of spontaneous humour. When he greeted you, when he looked at you, when he talked with you, it was always with a half smile on his face. It was his sense of humour which procured him a quick entrance into many a man's life and heart. It was his sense of humour which made the hostile under- graduate, hauled for cutting lectures or chapels, forget his hostility and the presence of the don ; though at the end of the interview he, probably for the first time, began to think whether chapel-going had any meaning, whether a lecture, if listened to, might conceivably profit the listener. It was his sense of humour which made all feel at home with him, which at the first attracted the most unlikely men, which inspired with confidence the shyest, and made the most frivolous and thoughtless not afraid of him. Yet while he would laugh, and make us laugh, for as long as ever any one wished, through all his unaffected merriment he made men feel the strange earnestness of his life. And all knew that, while he never obtruded on us religious or even serious matters, he was ready at a moment's notice to speak with us of spiritual things. And most men felt something of what a friend of his wrote of him after his death : " He understood of 'the things that matter' more than any man that I shall ever meet." And many men who owe to Forbes Robinson their first serious thoughts of and their first insight into " the things that matter " must feel the same. It is this fact that makes it impossible to measure the far-reaching deep influence of his life. For the greatness of that life lay not in any large influence on any large body of undergraduates, though the undergraduate life of Christ's College must, as a whole, have felt his real influence ; nor was his life great simply because he was a scholar and a thinker. But his life was great, and will for all time remain great, because it was an inspiration—there is no other word : it was, and is, a lasting, vivid, real inspiration to a few. What Bishop Westcott did on a large scale, Forbes Robinson did on a small. He inspired men—inspired them to search for and hold to the realities of life.

'To sum up : a man admitted into the inner chamber of his life learnt there something of these three things : (*a*) The value of his own personality, (*b*) the meaning of love, (*c*) the power of prayer.

E

'*a. The value of his own personality.*—A man, as he talked with Forbes, was taught with increasing clearness the amazing possibilities of life for any one who has tried to think what it means to say that " this is I." Many of us, conscious in ourselves only of very ordinary attainments, of no very high ideals, of weaknesses of character, learnt from our friend that in spite of all this, our own personality was God's greatest gift to us. We learnt from him that our own particular commonplace life was, with all its failures and inconsistencies, a tremendous enterprise, big with opportunities. He taught us this by his belief in us. He held (again like Bishop Westcott) through everything to the faith of " man naturally Christian." By his belief in a man he forced him at last to believe in himself. For he taught us that we were, each one, two men—the real " Ego " and the false—and that the real self must in the end have the mastery over the false, because that real self was the Christ.

'*b. The meaning of love.*—It is impossible for lesser natures to enter into all that the word " love " meant to Forbes. His love for his friends was " wonderful, passing the love of women." He loved some men with an intensity of feeling impossible to describe. It was almost pain to him. If he loved a man he loved him with a passionate love (no weaker expression will do). We undergraduates found our natures too small to understand it. Yet, as we learnt to know him more and more, we began too to learn a little of what real love is—we began to learn what can be the meaning and the wonder and the power and the depth of the love of man for man. And we understood in time that his love for us and his belief in us sprang from the same high source—from the Christ in him, in us.

'*c. The power of prayer.*—This last lesson explained the other two. Perhaps only a few of those who knew Forbes as undergraduates learnt it. Yet an intimate knowledge of him must have forced almost any man to the belief that 'more things are wrought by prayer than this world dreams of.' He prayed for those he loved, it is certain, for hours at a time. All his thoughts about some men gradually became prayers. He could not teach us everything that prayer meant to him ; he could not teach us to pray as he prayed. Yet through him one or two at least of his undergraduate friends saw a little further into the eternal mystery of prayer. And men must sometimes—with all reverence be it said—have experienced in his presence the same kind of a feeling of some great unseen influence at work as that which the disciples must have experienced in the presence of Christ after He, apart and alone, had watched through the night with God in prayer. For many an hour of his life did Forbes spend like that, striving with God for those he loved. He believed—he knew (this was his own testimony)—that he could in this way bring to bear upon a man's life more real effective influence than by any word of direct personal teaching or advice. So did he prove once more that the man of power in the spiritual world is the man of prayer.

' These are the great lessons of Forbes Robinson's

life—lessons which many a careless undergraduate learnt in a greater or less degree, and, learning, caught from the teacher something of his passion for life and love and prayer, for service of God and man.

'There must be many who will not soon forget the lessons ; there must be many in whose lives the influence and inspiration of that saintly life will be for ever a power making for holiness and high ideals of living ; there are, it is certain, very many who will thank God continually that they were, in their undergraduate days, allowed to call Forbes Robinson friend.

'How many of us, when we heard with a shock of almost horror that he had passed from us, conjured up before us the picture we shall never see again—the picture of our friend sitting any evening at his table in Darwin's historic rooms at Christ's, dimly lighted with candles ! We shall remember long the quick look up at our entrance, the half-smile on his face, the welcome of a man's love in his eyes, however busy and tired he might be. Then, though it cost him later hours out of bed, the invitation to sit down, followed quickly by an indignant remonstrance as we ousted his cat from the best arm-chair. And then the talk that followed : sometimes almost trivial ; sometimes (but only if we wished it) deeply serious ; sometimes—and these occasions were precious—a kind of soliloquy on his part, as he spoke of God, of the realities of life, of love, of prayer. Then, with still the same half-smile, he would bid us " Good night," and watch us out of the room with the same look of love in his eyes with which he welcomed us as he turned back to his table to work and think and pray far into the night.

'So many a one of us has left him again and again, to return to the merry, careless, selfish undergraduate world a nobler, better man. And now he has passed from us—" dead ere his prime " we should say, did we not understand that somewhere the faithful, hopeful, loving soul has better work to do. He is, as he ever was, " in Christ." He lives. His life remains here and beyond. His faith in God, in prayer ; his hope for every man ; his utterly wonderful, amazing love,—they still remain. For νυνὶ μένει (nothing can rob us of the word) πίστις, ἐλπίς, ἀγάπη, τὰ τρία ταῦτα· μείζων δὲ τούτων ἡ ἀγάπη.

LETTERS

To A. V. R.

Brislington Hill, Bristol : September 24, 1890.

. . . I have been persuaded to try the Semitic Languages Tripos. I have been learning German and Syriac a little this Long with that aim in view. . . . I don't really know what to do. I am trying to do what will best fit me for my future work. It is hard to know what is right.

. . . The only thing I want is not to develop into a mere bookworm. . . . The atmosphere of Cambridge so tends to deaden one, and to make one unsympathetic with humanity ; and yet the Church to-day does so need men who know something, men who can express with no uncertain sound the truth of Old Testament and New Testament criticism. I want so to find out what the Old Testament is, and how far we can believe in it, in its essential truth, in its historical accuracy. The question can only be settled by scholars—by scholars filled with the spirit of humility and understanding. It cannot be settled by the so-called spiritual faculty alone, but only by the intellect guided by the Spirit of Truth.

I have been reading St. John's Gospel in Greek and Syriac, and more and more I become convinced

that what it says is truth : ζωή—life—anything worth
calling life—anything that can last—anything that is
of use here and hereafter—is to be gained alone by
actually eating and drinking the Body of the Son of
Man. The expression is awfully strong—the expression in itself. I am not talking of all sorts of
modern explanations of the expression. Take it as
it stands in the original : 'You have no life, unless
you eat and drink. . . .'

I wish there could be a small Greek Testament
reading in the College for considering what the New
Testament really means, apart from modern interpre-
tations. Is it possible to find out the true, original
meaning of that book, and to understand its problems
a little and its solutions ? 'Quid importat scientia
sine timore Dei ?'

To T. H. M.

Aldeburgh House, Blackheath : March 20, 1891.

I am gradually finding out how ignorant I am
of the meaning of the New Testament, and how
miserably I have read my own miserable notions and
glosses into the words of St. Paul. I am sure that
the solution of the greatest problems which concern
humanity is to be found in his Epistles, if we could
only approach them without bias and with more
childishness. I feel certain that the Incarnation is
the great fact of the world's, and probably of the
universe's, history. 'The Word was made flesh.'

> And so the Word had breath, and wrought
>   With human hands the creed of creeds
>   In loveliness of perfect deeds,
> More strong than all poetic thought.

The death on Calvary must have had effects far beyond this particular world. 'He descended into hell.' He claimed His power over all parts of His universe. The Good *has* conquered. The Bad *is* defeated.

To T. H. M.

Christ's College, Cambridge : July 18, 1891.

We have but lately heard that my missionary brother[1] has passed away into the eternal world. He died in Africa. He gave up all, he gave up his life for Christ. Terribly as we feel the loss, and shall feel it still more, I cannot help thanking the Eternal Father that He has accepted the life-sacrifice, and feeling that He calls upon us here and now, each day and moment of our lives, to offer up ourselves on the altar of universal thanksgiving. Life is sacrifice, renunciation : true life is dependence on God. Sin is isolation, death—a failure to recognise and act on our dependence. I do feel as I seldom felt before something of the love of the Father, the grace of the Son, the communion of the Spirit. We *must* learn that an individual hope, aspiration, ambition, is against the law of the universe—the law of self-sacrifice. We *must* learn that our wills are ours to make them God's ; that if we have a single hope or thought which He does not inspire, which true humanity cannot share, the hope and thought are wrong. God grant that you and I may renounce

[1] John Alfred Robinson, formerly a scholar of Christ's College, who died at Lokoja on the River Niger, on June 25, 1891.

our individual lives, and become truly ourselves by martyrdom, by allowing the Christ in us to live.

I am to be ordained in September. Pray for me. There is no power like prayer. Let us pray for one another. The great Father longs for simple lives, simple piety, perpetual thanksgiving. And we have so much to be thankful for—so much here and now. I do long to offer body, mind, soul, affections, will, hope, to Him as a thanksgiving. Self-renunciation, life in a Church, a Body, is the only life. God grant we may live it !

To T. H. M.

Christ's College, Cambridge : November 17, 1891.

Do you know that it isn't a bad thing to feel a babe ? We must all become simple little children before we enter the kingdom of heaven, because God, who lives in that kingdom, has the simplest heart in all the wide universe—the most childlike, for God is Love. He has no cross purposes. Though He is stronger and better and bigger than we are, He is simpler. He will love a poor, simple old woman in His simple way with a wonderful affection. He is so simple, because He does not know what sin is. God never sins. God is Light, and in Him is no darkness at all.

It is this simplicity, this love of One who is omnipotent, uncreate, illimitable, eternal, that makes me reverence Him, adore Him, live for Him, love Him.

Simplicity is wonderfully attractive. The man who knows least of sin is most helpful to me, because he is most simple and Godlike. The 'man of the world' is most repulsive, because he is most like the Devil.

To E. N. L., on the occasion of his ordination.

Cambridge : March 10, 1892.

It gives me great pleasure to think that on Sunday next you will be made a Deacon in God's Church. I thank God that He has called you to one of the highest offices on earth, that henceforth you will be 'in' or (shall we say?) 'under' orders—God's orders —that you willingly renounce your life, your thoughts, your hopes, your ambitions to Him. You will probably hear much and be told much at this time. I have nothing to say that you have not heard and will not hear said far better by others. Our Church gives the keynote in the collect for Sunday : 'We have no power.' I never realised my weakness, my pride, my hollowness so much as I did at my ordination. God has been teaching me, even in the short time since I was ordained, wonderful lessons—lessons of strength being perfected in weakness. He alone knows the depths of our hypocrisy, our vanity, our atheism, and He alone can help us. To get nearer to Him, to know Him better—this is what I want, this is eternal life. As we believe in a Person who is by our side, who is helping us, training us, we shall be able to proclaim Him to others. Do not mind about feelings. You may have beautiful feelings at your ordination time. Thank God if you have. He sends them. You may have none. Thank God if you have not, for He has kept them back. We do not want to *feel* better and stronger; we want to *be* better and stronger. And He *has* made us better and stronger. He has given us His Spirit as we knelt before the bishop. We must go forth in that strength. We must use it, live on it, and it will be ours. Κατὰ τὴν πίστιν ὑμῶν γενηθήτω ὑμῖν. When we feel most hopeless, most wretched, most distant from God, remember 'feelings don't matter.' Remember that God's Son felt the same temptation, remember that He too was forsaken by His God. And when all seems lost, Satan seems master, we are misunderstood; remember that 'I believe in the Holy Ghost,' who is stronger than separation or death, than feelings, than our hearts. All our feelings and thoughts and wishes are nothing. God is everything and in all. All our conceptions will be shattered, all our schemes overthrown, that a Great Person behind may be revealed. To know, to love, to make known, to make men love that Person is our work in life . . . .

We are men sent from God. We come to bear witness of a Light. Do not let us confuse ourselves with our message. The message is everything; we are nothing. The Light simply shines through us. We must be glad to be shattered, rejected, if so be that the Light shining through us may be manifested.

One suggestion I make: that you do what I believe you are expected by the words of the Prayer-book to do—say the Morning and Evening Prayer daily *always*, unless you are ill, at home or in church, and the Litany on Wednesday, Friday, and Sunday. You will find this a greater help than almost anything else—a help against superstition, narrowness, bigotry, heartlessness. If you decide not to do so, do it with some *really* good reason, and not because others do the same, or because it is a bother.

And now good-bye. And may God grant us to know Him on earth, so that we may together know Him better hereafter.

To W. A. B.

Blackheath : April 20, 1892.

. . . No amount of philosophical theories are worth much compared with a simple picture of home life. It is these common relations of life which are most awful and sacred. The highest life we know is, I think I may say with reverence, family life—life of Father and Son ; family life on earth is a faint picture of something better in heaven. We shall be surprised some day to find that, while we have been searching for the noble and divine, we have it all the while at home. The relations of brother and brother, son and father, are eternal realities, which we shall never fathom, for God Himself is below them. 'Omnia exeunt in mysterium,' as Kingsley says in 'Yeast.' I am very pleased with that novel. The description he gives of the sufferings and squalor of villages is positively awful. We do want men who believe that self-sacrifice, not selfishness, is at the top of all, who are sure that family life is made in heaven and is made in the image of God's life, who know that in the present is the eternal, to go and live and work and die in our villages. But Kingsley shows it is not enough to give alms or other social benefits— we must do more than that, we must raise their whole

life and condition.   I believe myself that this can only
be done *from inside*.   Thus, when God wished to
redeem man, He did it from inside.   Man himself
fought and conquered.   Deity entered into humanity.
It is not merely that we must live simply, think
simply, work, as they do.   That is well, but we
must do more.   If we want to look at them from the
inside, I know only one way—the old, old way which
God Himself adopts.   We must love them, love the
Christ, the Spirit in them—not the beast, the devil in
them.   Like attracts like.   To love and to detect
that, we must have some of that Spirit, that Christ.

That means to say that to help others from the
inside, we must be right inside ourselves.   And yet
none of us are right inside.   But there is that in us
which is right, that in us which is not ourselves, but
is deeper than ourselves.   A Son who will make us
true sons, a Brother who will teach us how to be
brothers, a Human Being who will show us what is
in all human beings ; a Love who will teach us what
we always fancy we know, but what we don't know
(else we should be divine)—how to love ; a Man who
will make us saints and gentlemen—the Man Christ
Jesus.   Yes, and there is in us a Great Spirit who is
uniting us by invisible bonds to all that is good and
healthy and Godlike, a Spirit who disciplines our
will when it is weakest and most self-indulgent, who
trains our spirit and fights our battles against the
evil spirit, a Person who makes us persons.   How
then do men differ?   If in every man there is the
Light which lightens him, the Christ, the Spirit, what
is the difference between good and bad men ?   Does

a good man possess religion, or faith, or love? No, the best men would tell you they were possessed by faith and love, rather than that they possessed them. What faith or love they have is not a possession—it is in them, not of them, not belonging to them. It comes from the Christ in them. The difference between men is not that one is inspired and another is not, but that one yields to the Spirit, another does not. We begin to obey when we *lose* ourselves in that Spirit and forget all but God. We ought never to settle any detail in life without taking Him into account: we are fools if we do. How can we be logical? For He is in that detail, and not to think of Him is not to understand that detail. For every detail is more than a detail—it is the expression of a Person.

I have wandered into a train of thought suggested by 'Yeast,' and in part copied directly from it. Forgive me. I was half thinking aloud. That is my one excuse for saying what I am trying to think.

I never played golf. I do that sort of thing by deputy. K—— is the sort of man to do it for me. At any rate, I trust him with my football and rowing. It doesn't tire you so much if you do it that way. Only let me give you one piece of advice, which I only wish I acted upon: 'Don't do your thinking by deputy:' do your rowing, golf, football, cricket, skittles, talking if you like, but not your thinking.

To D. D. R., written apropos of a discussion on
St. Paul's idea of the relation between Sin and
the Law.

2 New Square, Cambridge :
Monday before Easter, 1892.

I cannot but help feeling that part of your difficulties are self-made.   Is there such a difference
between Jewish law and law in general ?   What is
law—law in the abstract ?   What do you mean when
you talk about laws of science or morality ?   Surely
there is no such thing as law in the abstract.   You
really mean God's thought.   All law existed long
before this world existed, as the thought of God.
This thought expresses itself, when the world is
actually made, in animals, nature, man.   But this
thought is somewhat long before it expresses itself,
because it is God's thought.   With Him 'to think' is
'to do.'   Before you and I were born, before men
were made, man exists in God as a thought.   Each
of us is an expression of part of that thought.   The
whole thought is the image of God, not any one part.
Now, when I speak of man as something in contradistinction to men, I mean the thought of God in
contradistinction to its individual realisation.   So
when I speak of law as distinct from special laws,
I mean a thought of God as distinct from its special
expressions.   Otherwise ' man ' and ' law ' are abstractions and nonentities.

The nominalist is right in so far as he denies that
law as an abstract thing (considered apart from a
person—as his thought) is anything : the realist is
right in so far as he affirms that law, apart from

any particular manifestation, is an eternal reality.
The reconciliation of nominalism and realism is
found in God. Applying this to the case in hand
—you admit that the Ten Commandments are the
ground of morality ; therefore, I say, they must be
an expression of a thought of God, the Author of
morality. But you are puzzled to find that the
most trivial sanitary arrangements are considered
by the Jew as equally a manifestation of God. Need
we be ? In every little sanitary precaution I recognise, or ought to recognise, an expression of that
same mind as I see it in the Ten Commandments.
God is Light, therefore the clean, the healthy, the
decent is an expression of Him. God is Love, therefore the social, the self-sacrificing, is an expression of
Him as well. But sanitary arrangements and the
like, though an expression of an unchanging principle, change according to state of civilisation, climate,
country. Therefore we take the principle, not the
expression, as the ultimate reality in the case of these
sanitary laws.

I am afraid I am rather stupid, and cannot make
my meaning plain. I want to show you that the
Jewish law only differs from English law as being
in some ways a more complete expression of God's
nature. But in all sanitary law, &c., *now* we have
God's nature expressed. And it would be true to
say, ' God spake unto England, saying '—*e.g.* in a
right decision in court ; it would be true to say,
'God spake unto the judge, saying.' Therefore,
what holds good of Moses' law holds good of all
law, because all law is a thought of God. There-

fore St. Paul uses indifferently νόμος and ὁ νόμος, for what is true of God's thought is true of every expression of it. In fact, he more often perhaps argues about one particular expression of it. Why? Because we can only tell what the thought is by studying the expression.

Don't be taken in by abstractions. An ideal is nothing—worse than nothing—unless our ideal is God's idea. Then it is the only reality, because God's idea will take effect. His idea is to make man in His image, and be sure it will take effect. Commandments, judgments, statutes, mean much the same in the Old Testament, I conceive, as we mean when we use them. The Ten Commandments are not so called in the Bible, I think. They are called ' words,' I think.

I do not think St. Paul at all restricted νόμος to the Ten Commandments. In fact, I don't know that he ever very clearly separated those off from all the rest.

Do not in your essay make the same mistake as many of the Jews in St. Paul's time. Do not try to consider law apart from the Law-giver. They looked upon law as a dead thing by itself, not as an expression of the character of a person.

Thus the Commandment about resting on the Sabbath day was considered by them as an order as though from a tyrant. But God, when He gave it, did not simply say, ' Here it is : do it '—but ' Do it because,' and He gives the reason why. The reason is different in Exodus and Deuteronomy, because the books were, to a certain degree perhaps, written to

F

illustrate different aspects of God's character. Exodus says : 'Work and rest, because God's life is work and rest. Therefore human life made in His image is work and rest.' Deuteronomy says : 'Work and rest. God has emancipated you from slavery. He bids you rest.' In both cases God is the ground of the law. Study law—any law—English law—and in so far as it is law, and not lawlessness under guise of law, you will be studying God Himself ; for if St. Paul's principles are true at all, they must be true of all law. But, oh ! don't deal with abstractions, which sound well, but mean little. Let us use what we have. It is a grand thing to know that the highest ideal we can conceive must be realised, for the highest ideal must be part of God's idea.

Don't try to look at moral law apart from national life. St. Paul did not. Law is seen in national life. A nation is a better expression of God than an individual, because God is three, not simply one. He is a social Being, a Being of relations. And nations will last for ever. Law will always be seen worked out in national life. God has more worlds than one. Each nation is a thought of God worked out in human clay (cf. Jeremiah xviii. 1–6). Human clay lasts for ever (' I believe in the resurrection of the body'). Law will always be worked out thus. We are part of a thought of God—part of an English nation—little fragments of a huge whole. Our immortality depends on the fact that we are parts of a nation, parts of a Divine idea, which lasts for ever. Law is more completely seen in conscious than unconscious life, because God's life is conscious. Law is more completely seen

In family and national than individual life, because in God Himself are seen the archetypes of human relations.

This letter is disjointed, but contains a few thoughts which may prove helpful—thoughts I have been learning from others of late.

We are having lovely weather.

The buds 'feeling' after each other—new life and resurrection life—a type, a pledge of fuller resurrection, of Easter life—nay, the same Life—' I am the Resurrection and the Life'—working in trees and flowers and man. What a glorious thing to live in a world which has been united with its Maker—a world of perfect law and order—a world where every infraction of law must and will be punished—a world where Love is Law and Law is Love—a world where a great thought is being realised, and will be realised in and for us! You use 'Theology' loosely— 'Theology' is *the* thing and 'Religion' is not, I think, nearly such a fine word. Theology is the Learning, Knowing, Studying God. I am sorry I have said nothing about Jewish sacrificial law. I meant to. That expresses a great fact. It dimly hints (as sacrificial law in other nations does) at the fact that the ground of the universe is self-sacrifice—that the ground of all human, whether family or national, life is a filial sacrifice. I think other nations besides Jews regarded *all* law as coming from God ; nay, I think all nations did in part at least.

*To E. N. L., on the occasion of the death of his brother,
who was killed by lightning at Cambridge.*[1]

June 18, 1892.

. . . I do feel for you, and could do a great deal to
help you. I can only tell you what I have felt to
be the only thing which makes life endurable at a time
of real sorrow—God Himself. He comes unutterably
near in trouble. In fact, one scarcely knows He exists
until one loves or sorrows. There is no 'getting over'
sorrow. I hate the idea. But there is a 'getting
into' sorrow, and finding right in the heart of it the
dearest of all human beings—the Man of Sorrows, a
God. This may sound as commonplace, but it is
awfully real to me. I cling to God. I believe He
exists. If He does not, I can explain nothing. If
He does, all whom we love are safer with Him than
with us. If we can only get nearer ourselves to God,
we shall get nearer to those whom we love, for they
too are in God.

We shall be one, ever more and more really one,
the nearer and the liker we get to God. . . . My dear
friend, words are poor comfort at a time like this, when
we see into eternity. A Person is our only hope, and
that Person is God. God often takes those whom He
loves best home to Himself as soon as He can. In
the process of their development they break through
the bonds of space and time. He has taken your
brother, but not taken him away from you. We are

[1] Writing to another friend at this time he says, ' He was walking
with a friend, and in a moment, without any apparent pain, " God's
finger touched him and he slept." '

all in the same home—praying for, knowing, loving each other. . . I believe in the communion of saints— I believe that those who began to know God here, and whom we call dead, are not dead. They are just beginning to live, because they are finding out God : they are just beginning to know us, because they see us as we are—they see us in God. They are with Jesus, and Jesus is a human being. Because they are with a human being, a man, *the* man, the Son of man, they must, they do, take a deep interest in the affairs of the sons of men, and—may we not believe ?—in us, whom they knew below. . . .These are truths which sorrow helps me to make my own. I pray that you may never, never 'get over' the sorrow, but get through it, into it, into the very heart of God.

To A. W. G.

Blackheath : June 27, 1892.

I have more and more come to the conclusion for some time past that the only reality underlying and explaining the world must be personal. I know that I am a person, and that it is persons—especially a few particular persons—not things, who have influenced me and had a power in my life. All my ideas of justice and purity and goodness are inseparably bound up with persons. At last I have come to the conclusion that nothing exists except the personal, and that below all is One who is personal. That means to say that the world and things in it are only real in so far as they are thoughts of God. We are real only in so far as we are thoughts of God. A

Roman Catholic poet, speaking of the Virgin Mary, says :

> If Mary is so beautiful,
> What must her Maker be?

I look round the world and I see persons who attract me in a wonderful way—persons who are more gracious and simple than I am ; and then I cannot help feeling that they all are a kind of faint picture of One who is better than all of them, One in whose image they are made. I like, I cannot help liking, intensely some of them ; and from them I am led on to Him who made them and who therefore must— if I only knew Him—be more attractive even than they are. I believe that we are intended to rise from them to Him who made them, that if we stop short with the creature, we lower ourselves—we become idolaters. We worship beauty or intellect or good- ness as though they belonged to the creature ; we thereby lower ourselves and the persons whom we worship. If, on the contrary, we rise from them to the Personal Being, we see more in them than we ever saw before, and we get nearer to them than we ever got before. For life is a circle whose centre is God. Each of us is unconnected with his neighbour, but connected with the centre from whom he comes. The nearer the centre, the nearer we get to each other. When we get to the centre, we really become united with each other. To die is to get a step nearer the centre. The closer we are connected with the centre, the nearer we are to those whom we call dead. Our communion with them is spiritual, be- cause ' God is spirit ' and they are in Him. But the spiritual is not the unsubstantial, the nebulous, the gaseous ; it is the personal—to my mind the awful—reality. The more truly we understand persons, the more we shall find they are spirits.

I tell you what has been the greatest possible strength to me of late. God is not merely a Person, He is Three Persons in One. I am always trying to get closer to those whom I love best, to know them more, to serve them better. Yet something is ever keeping us apart. I said 'something,' I mean 'some one,' for only a person can keep a person from another—only a malicious, a devilish person—yet I feel that some day I shall be able to love, and know them better. Then I look out on life and I see how again and again death, and some one worse than death, is separating us, misinterpreting motives, keeping men apart ; men are struggling to be one, and cannot be ; on earth persons long to be one, persons who love feel they ought to be, they must be one. In heaven Three Persons are really, perfectly, quite One. What we are trying to do has been done there. Men try to be one. God is One. And the comfort comes in when one knows that 'in the image of God made He man.' Our life is a copy ; God's life is the original. Because God is One, we, whose life is a picture of His, shall some day be one, as He is. The unity of Deity is a pledge of the unity of humanity.

The more we make our life like the original the more shall we realise what we long to realise—truer, deeper, more eternal unity. But we are not simply *trying* to be, we *are* one. All we have to do, I believe, is to act as though we were one. We have proofs of this unity. We find ourselves doing an action which we should never have done unless we had known some one. That one lives over his life, or part of his life, again in us. So too we are living over our lives in other people, perhaps in some who have passed into other worlds of fuller activity than this. In living our lives over in each other, we show that we are more than we thought ; and it is grand to think how big our lives may become in this way, for those whom we *influence*—into whom our life *flows in*—in turn may influence others. When I get quite quiet, and my mind is sane, and my conscience at rest, when I almost stop thinking, and listen, I am quite sure that a Personal Being comes to me, and, as He comes, brings some of His own life to flow into my life. I am also sure that with Him come those who live in Him, that all whom I have known or know, and longed or long to know better, who were *worth* knowing, are near me, are, if I let them, living their lives in my life, making me what I should not be without them. (These are facts, of which I think I may say I have more certainty in the best moments of my life than I have now that Switzerland exists. But I may be exaggerating. Perhaps as regards the second fact—of the other persons with Him—I may have spoken too strongly as regards my certainty. It is so hard to say *exactly* what one means.)

I don't know that these thoughts will be of much use to you. They may sound somewhat too philosophical. But I have more or less purposely put them in a philosophical form, because we are not thus so easily led astray into vague pleasant feelings, which we sometimes get from rhetoric. But I do wish I could put a little more of my feelings into this cold paper, and cruel, unsympathetic ink. For what I have written is not a mere philosophy of life ; it is the only thing that makes life tolerable for a moment to me ; it is the one thing which I intensely long to realise. To my mind life is love, and love is life. Love is not sentimental affection, simply the readiness to die for a person. But love is the laying down of life for a person, absolutely renouncing your life for another. It means living the best life you can conceive of for the sake of one you love ; knowing for certain that your life is flowing into that other person, though you may never see him again in this world. Love is purifying yourself that another may be pure. Love for one person, if it be true love, leads you at once to God, for ' God is Love.' I do not know what that means, but I do know that the little meaning I can see in it explains everything. As we love, God is there ; we see God, we are in God. So we are led on from unselfish love on earth to that unselfish family life of Three in One in heaven ; we are led on to Him in whose image we are made, and whose image we never so clearly reflect as when we love most. I could go on talking on this subject almost for ever, but I think I had better not tax your patience.

To W. A. B.

Christ's College, Cambridge : July 5, 1892.

How very jolly for you to get out right away into the country ! I hope some day to be able to do the same. But I think, on the whole, *I* am better suited for retiring from the world than you are ! If it were right to wish it, I might almost wish to exchange places with you. But yet I don't. It is very curious—I dare say you have thought of it—how very, very few people, if any, you would deliberately wish to change into, if you could. One admires many people, and would like to have their goodness, their intellect, or their beauty or strength—but how few of them one would really *be* : to cease at once to be yourself, and suddenly to be some one else—to look at life with *their* eyes, to have *their* past, *their* hopes for the future, *their* sins, *their* inmost thoughts, *their* anxieties. There is only about one man in the world, whom I know, whom I would like to be—and even of that I am not sure. It is the wonderful sense of personality. We abuse 'me' ; we often vaguely say we would rather be some one else ; yet very few of us wish to lose 'me' : and most of us perhaps never will.

Liddon is, I should think, somewhat stiff and uninteresting. Gore's Bampton Lectures on much the same subject are far more interesting to my mind, far more human. Lectures IV, V, VI of Gore would perhaps interest and educate you on the subject.

Are you so sure that your course at Cambridge is ' over ' ?

> I looked behind to find my past,
> And lo, it had gone before.

You will find traces of that course, before you have done, in yourself and in others for good or for evil. It is a good thing to think that nothing good is ever 'over'—that whatever we do is done for eternity, is part of ourselves and of others—that we live on in others, live on a nobler life than we lived in ourselves. When we *influence* another, our life *flows into* another : we live our life over again in him. The day will come when we shall see more clearly into what we have been doing. As yet we are like children playing with knives : they little know how near they are to killing themselves at times. So we are playing with big issues : we call them small and secular, we treat them as such—yet every speck of dust is big with infinity. Would that we could see the Infinite Being at every turn, then we should begin to live. You will get wrong in all your plans unless you see them in Him, and Him in them, and correct them as you see them thus—correct your thoughts to fit in with His thoughts, not His thoughts to fit in with your thoughts.

But you'll learn it is true. You'll understand later on why I am always talking about a Person ; why to know that Personal Being is life. Meanwhile, thank you very, *very* much for what you have taught me. I feel I am down in the bottom class of that school, but I am glad that I have got into the school at all. Later on I may reach a higher standard, and know the Teacher better. In that school the lesson each of us is set to learn is love, and the name we are all trying to spell out is the name of the Father and of the Son and of the Holy Spirit. Some of us, perhaps, have learnt to spell one part of the name, some of us another. But none of us have properly learnt to love one single person as we ought ; and few of us have learnt to see the Father's love in all, the Son's grace in all, and the Spirit's fellowship in all. But patience must have her perfect work : and if we work hard at our lessons, we shall know more, love more, think in a simple way, and *do* more. But we must not be learning merely from each other ; the pupils must look away to the Master of all in the centre, and as we all learn from Him and love Him, we shall be more modest, there will be no competition—save who can love most and sacrifice most— and do most for Him who has done all for us.

This letter is hurried. Forgive it. Write again. Accept the will for the deed. Think, think, think !

To T. H. M.

Ivy House, Holkham : September 1, 1892.

The sacraments are tremendous realities to me, just because they are a living protest against all Popish, High Church, Low Church schemes of thought—because they are a protest that man does nothing, God does all—that everything is a sacrament of the grace of God. They explain all life to me. They teach me what love means, for when man might least expect it, love comes deluging in, and the outward and visible is overwhelmed with the inward and spiritual. Oh, if bread and wine and water are capable of being transformed into the highest means of grace and hopes of glory ; may not living, human, breathing persons—may not those

I love—be sacraments as well? When we come near human beings we love, we should come with the same feelings of reverence as when we kneel at that altar, for we are coming to that which is part of God's image—made in His likeness. And as we speak to them, when they answer purely and simply, the Word of God speaks through them. This is not degrading the sacraments—nay, but raising all human life— nay, raising the sacraments as well, for it brings them into relation with real life, and transforms the poor magical abstractions into eternal realities.

To W. A. B., who had told him that he had made up his mind to take up school work till he was old enough to be ordained.

Holkham : September 3, 1892.

A home circle reminds me, I think, more than anything else of that other home, that other family— the home of a Father and of a Son, the family circle of the Three who live in one unity. We should thank God for every family circle on earth into which we are allowed to enter, and in whose life He allows us to share—for any true family on earth—yes, and every little child who is born into this strange world of ours is a sure and certain pledge—a real sacra- ment—that God loves us still, has not forgotten us, is giving us little glimpses into His own family life, is making existence here a more perfect image of life in heaven. We should come into such a family circle with the same feelings of awe as when we bend on our knees to receive the Holy Communion. For here, too, we enter into Holy Communion—the communion of simple, human, happy family life ; here, too, we approach a sacrament, outward and visible signs of happy, quiet, home life—the signs of an inward and spiritual grace—the grace which lies below and interprets all human grace in man and woman— the grace of our dear Lord and Saviour Jesus Christ. True, that grace is but little realised in the best of families—little consciously realised in the noblest life. But, oh ! surely a human family—brothers and sisters in a home on earth—are a sure and certain pledge that this grace does exist—that God is—for here we have an exquisite though imperfect copy of the family life of God. Thank God when you see a good or a beautiful man or woman, a pure and a simple family —thank God, because it is a revelation, a manifestation, an unveiling, a copy, a likeness of Himself. For though beauty often is proud and trivial, yet it is a manifestation of Him from whom all beauty comes, in whom all beauty dwells, by whom all beauty exists. And so not only thank—pray. Pray to Him that the outward and visible may be ever more and more but an expression of something inward and unseen and spiritual. For beauty, grace, intellect, everything is doomed, unless it is sacramental—unless it draws its life from God below, unless it lives but to testify of Him who is.

It is an awful problem—a beautiful face with no true moral beauty below—splendid physical grace with no deeper grace beneath—a strong, capable intellect which is not the expression of a noble soul. What does it all mean ? How in a world, where the outward and visible is but a manifestation of the

good God, can such awful anomalies exist? Partly
it is due to the law that goodness is rewarded to a
thousand generations (Exodus xx. 6. R.V. margin,
cf. Deut. vii. 9), while wickedness is visited upon
the third and fourth—that is, that one who is beautiful
in body or intellect, and who knows God, leaves the
blessing of such beauty long after him to descendants
who are little conscious of the reason of its origin,
and who have little thought of God.

Beautiful eyes, where there is no beauty of soul
beneath, are the eyes of others, long since dead, looking at us still—men who served God in their generation. An exquisitely touching voice, where there is
no music in the life of the one who possesses it, may
be the voice of one who knew God, and left his
legacy for a thousand generations. But still the
problem remains. In many cases the outward and
inward seem divorced. Now let us not try rashly to
solve the problem ourselves. We are inclined when
we see such beauty to say, 'It is no use talking. I
am quite sure, whatever you say, that there must be
some fine traits in the character of one whose face
is like the face of an angel, whose voice is sweeter
than that of the sons of men.' We may be, I believe
we are, partly right—at least in many cases, for the
spiritual powers of those who are gone may still in
part live on in their descendants. But often, if we
are candid, we must admit that apparently the outward and visible are separated from the inward and
spiritual, that we have outward beauty and grace
which is no sign at all of anything deeper—nay, that
the very spiritual qualities, of which it is the sign,

and which may once have existed in the person, have been used for the vilest ends. This being the case, we are still left with the problem, Is the outward and visible not intended to be a sign of something deeper? Here it is not a sign. Why not? Will it ever be so? To put the case in its short, simple, concrete form, how can a 'flirt' exist when by all the laws of the universe beauty should surely be a sign not of instability, insipidity, unspirituality, worldliness, shallowness, hypocrisy, but of the Supreme?

I cannot answer this question. I doubt whether any man can. But I can show you where its ultimate solution must lie. It lies in the sacraments. Yes, they are the answer to the whole problem. They tell us that the outward and visible—the commonest objects, water, wine, bread—may be the signs of something which is deeper than anything we know. And they tell us more. They are to my mind a sure and certain pledge that some day the outward and visible shall really correspond to the inward and invisible. For, remember, this world lasts for ever. The good lasts, and is purified by fire. The evil alone is consumed. The sacraments are a pledge to me that some day upon this world our longings after a correspondence of the inward with the outward will be fulfilled—how, God only knows—probably not in the way we expect, but in a way far, far better. For His thoughts are not our thoughts, and His ways are not our ways. When therefore you are utterly bewildered and perplexed by finding so much that is attractive which seems utterly divorced from God's life; when you find yourself that the outward and visible in your own life—the words you say, the actions you do, tend to become absolutely different from your real inward life ; when you feel that every one is a hypocrite, and you are the worst of all, kneel down at that wonderful service, and take what is the one power of making outward and inward correspond, of making our words a true index of our thoughts, our actions a true presentation of our lives ; kneel down and pray that all you love may enter more and more into the meaning of that service, that they too may flee from self to One who is stronger than self— to the power which is capable of transforming our actions—to the power which raised Christ from the dead, and is capable of raising us up also. Then you will gradually be taught that all life is of the nature of a sacrament—that all food is to be taken because thereby we have health and strength to manifest forth the grace of God in a too often graceless world—you will be taught lessons which I cannot even suggest ; for God knows so much more than any of us what unsearchable riches He has as an inheritance for us. Let us enter upon that inheritance. God has called us to be saints, called us, chosen us—chosen us before the world was made— He has chosen us that in us, through us, He might manifest Himself. It is not humility that prevents us recognising the fact. It is our selfishness and stupidity. For the very fact that He has called and chosen you and me and all His Church before we were born shows that everything comes from Him. *We* are utterly worthless and vile, but when united, as we *are* united to God, we are transformed into His

G

image, we partake of His life. Only let us be what we are—sons of God.

In regard to those words, 'I looked behind to find my past, and lo it had gone before,' I do not know whether you are right or wrong about the Greek idea. The past *has* gone before us, we are always coming upon it. Some day we shall be confronted with it. Every day that we live we are making something that we shall meet again. The only way to get unity into our lives—to make it possible to look back without sentimental repining or an awful sense of dread—is to get God as the centre, God as the foundation. As we look back then we shall find days 'linked each to each by natural piety' —we shall see that our life forms a connected whole a real progress, something worth calling life.

. . . Do you know that the best way to strengthen your best thoughts is to try and express them? Get them out; you help others, you help yourself. Don't be careful of the grammatical accuracy and the finish of your sentences; I don't think St. Paul was. I was thinking to-day that perhaps a man who never wrote letters never could appreciate St. Paul. He was a great letter-writer. Copy him. Read him. Read him fairly quickly. Get into him. Find out his motive power, his real meaning. Read the Greek, not from a critical point of view only, but read the Greek. Do not trouble too much about the dictionary and accurate translations, but keep reading and perhaps saying aloud the Greek. St. Paul knew so much of God. Read him, and as you read, a greater than St. Paul will come into you, interpret him, explain him. St. Paul himself will be with you, I think, trying to show you what he meant, and what he has found out that he means now.

But do write me a proper letter. We are just beginning life, and we have so much to learn from and to teach each other. Everything is new to us. Everything is strange. Already it seems to me I have been trained in a hard school—harder, I hope, than you will ever need to be trained in—to understand what God and love mean. I seem to have had a rough time of it, perhaps rougher than most ; and even now I am trained in a way which is not attractive to me, trained to throw myself not on any merely human love, but on Him who is perfectly human and perfectly divine. May God train you in a less rough school, if possible ! But at any rate, may He train you—train you to get out of self, bring you into deeper sympathies, stronger attachments, simpler earnestness ! He alone can give unity to all our thoughts and desires. He alone can give stability. And we poor little creatures, who seem to have twice as much affection as we have mind, how we do need that stability ! We want not to be blown hither and thither by every manifestation of strength, beauty, brain—we want to be able to enter into the meaning of what we see and cannot help admiring, without becoming the slaves of the visible and the finite. We must build on the one foundation that is laid. We must lay our affections deep down in the man Christ Jesus. As we see Him in men—and, when we cannot see that, see men in Him—we shall be more stable, less childish, less fickle. We never go deep enough. We skim over life. We must get into its heart. We must never begin an affection which can have an end. For all affection must draw us into God, and God has no end. The moment we see any one whose strength, grace, goodness, beauty, or simplicity attracts us, we have deathless duties by that person. For the attraction is the outward sign of a spiritual connection —a sign that we ought to pray for that person, to thank God for the manifestation of His character, which we see in a riddle, through a glass in that life, that human life.

And then we shall be prepared to realise deeper relationships, more wonderful mysteries of love—to see with clearer eyes the heart of the Supreme. We cannot make relationships too spiritual. We cannot be too careful to see them in God and God in them. Think what it is to see a relationship *in God*, to see it existing there in His life, as His thought, long, long before we were born, long before we had an idea that we were intended to realise it. What a new light on old relationships—brother and brother, brother and sister, father and child, husband and wife, all thoughts of God, all being gradually entered into, appropriated, realised, understood, worked out by us. They seem so common and natural, and yet they are intensely awful and sacred and mysterious. And then think what it is to see *God in them*—to see One from whom all family life flows, penetrating those whom we have never properly learnt to love and those whom we love as much as we can. God in them—all that is good and attractive—not their own, but God's. The eyes which seem to be contemplating something which we cannot see, the face which lights up at times with another than human light; the eyes, the face, a realisation and expression of that Being who is at once human and divine, God and man. Why, this is bringing heaven down to earth, this is a realisation in part of the holy city coming down from heaven. For as we think of them, above all as we pray for them, we are led beyond them, we forget our own selfish interests in them, we are brought out from the 'garden' life of individual souls into the 'city' corporate life of a great human society, a family, the Church of God. We should live, we should die for Christ and His Body—the Church—the fulness of His life, who is filling all in all. We must cease thinking and praying for ourselves and for others, as though we were alone. We are all part of one great society. Around us—nay, in us—are others, some whom we can see, some who in the course of development have burst the bonds of space and time and matter, all one, one, for ever one. We all have one common Lord, one common hope, one common life, one common enemy, one common Saviour, who is working through us, in us, in those whom we least understand, in those in whom we should least expect it, in those who are almost repulsive to us, in all—working out one big purpose through the ages, the purpose of the Eternal.

Remember me at my ordination as priest, please. Remember me, for I need it so much, you do not know how much. It is such an important time, and I cannot understand or enter into its significance, as I long to do. Discipline, discipline, discipline. self-discipline—obedience to 'orders.' Oh! how I long to have the power to realise these! Pray for me that I may ; that you may, pray also. Be very strict with yourself. Compel yourself to obey rules. You are hurting so many besides yourself when you are not strict with yourself. For we are 'one body.' You are injuring those whom you like best, for you have less power over them, when you have less power over yourself—less power to influence, to pray, to thank for them.

Do remember how marvellously sacred a school-master's work is : it is not enough to be able to play games—how I sometimes wish I could!—it is not enough to be able to teach Latin and Greek : a schoolmaster should be so much more. He repre-sents the authority of God. He can be *so* much, he may be *so* little to boys. We can never enter into a boy's life, into his deepest thoughts, his 'long, long thoughts,' unless we too become little children, unless we become young and fresh and simple—and all young life comes from Him, who makes all the little chil-dren who ever come into this big world. Let us enter into His life. Do not become a schoolmaster simply to fill up time, to have something to do.

To W. A. B.

Christ's College, Cambridge : November 20, 1892.

. . . I am glad that you like your school, that you like your boys. . . . Think of the weak chaps, those who are 'out of the way,' those who are not naturally attractive, those who positively repel you. They often most need your sympathy, your prayers.

And now about your ordination. Do you know I am doubtful whether it would be a good thing for you to be ordained to a school chaplaincy. I am almost more than doubtful. You would, I suppose, have no parish work, nor anything to do with poor folk. Your work would be reading prayers, and preaching about three times a year, I suppose. You would scarcely care to be a curate in a country or poor town parish later on, would you, if you began thus? But, after all, I must not, I dare not, advise you. I can only point you to the Being who alone can advise us. The great thing is to renounce all plans, all thoughts of self, to give up all we are and expect to be, to come into His presence, and then to ask His advice. Or rather we must come to Him like little helpless children and ask Him to *help* us to renounce planning and arranging with *self* as goal— to beg Him to give us strength to give up all.

The great thing is to get the life where we shall develop best all our powers—viz. the life in which we shall have most opportunities of sacrifice. Can you get, can you *use*, opportunities of self-sacrifice in your school life? Can you get fuller and better elsewhere? . . . Of course, if you find that you have more influence over boys than you would be likely to have over other folk, that might alter the case. Have you found that you can influence them more for good than you would be likely to influence others?

Our one work in life must be to advance God's glory, God's kingdom. The time is short. The night soon comes. The great problem is how to do most in that short time ; how we ourselves can best lose ourselves in the little time that we have for losing ourselves. 'He that loseth himself, findeth himself.'

To D. D. R.

14 St. Margaret's Road, St. Leonards: January 10, 1893.

I have been thinking to-day of that strange statement 'I no longer call you slaves . . . but I have called you friends.' To understand any one you must be their friend : you are able then to judge their life from the inside, to see why and how they do what they do ; all their actions which seemed disconnected and purposeless before are seen to be part of a plan, to have an end, a goal. We cannot understand the riddle of life, the necessity of all the details in the great scheme of redemption, the reason for certain means of grace, the real significance of the hope of glory, while we are slaves. The whole appears so purposeless, such waste of energy, such unintelligible and irrational self-sacrifice. Why must the Christ suffer ? Why could not sin be overcome in a less costly way ? Why is the victory of the Christ so incomplete ? Why do some, who are better than we, take so little interest in the eternal ? We cannot answer these and a thousand other questions while we are slaves. All is a hopeless enigma, a play without a plot, a novel with no plan. But become a friend of a man and all is changed. Each act in his life, each thought in his life, each word from his lips—they have not ceased to be a problem, they are ten thousandfold more wonderful than they ever were before : they are still a problem ; but there is, there must be, we feel, a purpose running through the whole. We have but one object—to understand him more, to see what divine ideal he is trying to work out in all the details of his common life. Each detail is important; each thought, however wayward, must be recognised and understood. All are seen in the clear, dry light of eternity ; each is seen in something like its right proportion. We feel that his life is our life—nay, more interesting than our own miserable life—that if we are ever to know ourselves we must know him first. So, too, become a friend of Him who alone is, and all is changed. Gradually, perhaps painfully, yet surely, as we become like very little children, the meaning of the whole dawns upon us. We see it all : we see that it could not be otherwise : we cannot say why, but we are quite sure that we see it—at least, we see a little way, and where the light ends and it begins to get dark, we feel that it is all right beyond—that He who is with us in the light will be with us in the darkness. We are no longer slaves, doing His will because we must. We are friends, and we cannot help taking deep interest in all that He does. His acts, His thoughts, His words, they are still a problem—we cannot make them all out. But they are the same kind of problem as a friend is—a strange exquisite torture. We do not know what the whole of his life means ; he can do things which we cannot, and which we rejoice to know that we can never do. We only see one side of him ever, and the rest is only known to God.

And yet we *do* know part of his life, and we are content to know no more ; what we know is good, and what we do not know or understand must also be good. We judge from what we see what that must be which we cannot see. We do not wish it otherwise. We feel that it would be impious to try and understand him fully, for is he not connected with God Himself? So we see one side of the life of the Eternal ; but we are friends ; we do not wish it otherwise. We cannot understand Him—we never can. And yet ' I have called you friends.' His main purposes we see : the plan by which He realises them we see in part. And as we know Him better, we shall be able to track His footsteps even where we did not expect to find Him. We shall learn that His methods are simpler and better than ours, that His thoughts are surer, deeper, higher than all our schemes and plans. I am constantly finding that ordinances, customs, beliefs, which I used to despise as strange, antiquated, or useless, are yet the very ones which I need, that my fathers knew better than I my needs, that above all God Himself had provided institutions and customs, and had waited until I was old enough to learn their use and to bless Him as I used them. So, as we know a man better, we feel that we must pray for him and his the more. As we become the friends of the Word, we feel we must pray that His will may be done ever more and more— His purposes realised by us and ours. Let us then not begin by criticising the world and God ; let us first be the friends of God, and then in the light of undying friendship and prayer begin to criticise.

We must be the friend of a man before we understand his life ; we must be the friends of Jesus Christ before we understand His life now upon earth.

I used to skate : I don't now. I obey herein one of the great maxims of my life : ' If you want to get a thing well done, *don't* do it yourself.' I consider that K——, in this as in other similar pursuits, performs the ancient and ' sacred duty of delegation.' I have no doubt that he does it admirably. Why must people try what they can't do well ? Why not leave it to those who like it and can do it well ? The wretched public-school-boy conception of dull uniformity is an abomination to me ! If K—— does the walking, you do the thinking ; G—— does the dandy, M—— the grumbling, S—— the jack-in-the-box, G—— the running, M—— the philosopher, and D—— the little vulgar boy—allow me to do what after all is the hardest of all tasks, ' to do nothing gracefully.' (I am afraid that I begin by trying ' to do nothing—gracefully,' but end by ' doing nothing gracefully.' You see the difference !) I believe in division of labour—let each man do what he is made to do best—and those who feel their vocation to be nothing but receiving the results of the labour of others—why, let them try to do it with the best grace they can ! Forgive me if such be my case.

To J. L. D

Christ's College, Cambridge : May 15, 1893.

I think you are right in believing in the intense worth of sympathy. But ' sympathy ' is the Greek

as 'compassion' is the Latin form of 'suffering together with.' He who has suffered most has perhaps
the most power to sympathise ; not simply to pity
or console, but to go right out of self and to get
right into another, to see life with his eyes, to feel
as he feels. If, then, you find many of those among
whom your lot is cast almost incapable of sympathy,
may it not be that they have not yet learned the
meaning of suffering ? They may not have had so
many opportunities of suffering as you, or, if they
have had as many, they may not have found any
one to interpret to them what it all meant. Thank
Him from whom all sympathy comes if you have
known anything of the sufferings of life, anything of
the worries and disappointments and delays and
unsatisfied ambitions which so many have ; if you
have known these—known their inner meaning, and
have been led out and beyond your own into that
wider life of suffering, and have learned what it is
to fill up in your turn τὰ ὑστερήματα τῶν θλίψεων
τοῦ Χριστοῦ.

One hates to see others whose centre is self.
Their whole life looks so mean and low. Life over,
the Ego alone left ; and what a poor, wretched,
snivelling creature after all—this which we pampered,
this which we thrust forward for others to admire and
flatter ! If we were not in much the same case, we
might be able to view it in others with somewhat
different eyes. And yet do you know that, as a
matter of fact, our Ego is dead—self is not—and the
devil's greatest lie is to make us believe in this self ?
For do not you and I belong to One stronger than

self—One whose own self may live in us—does live
in us—whether we recognise the fact or not? We
died years ago to self when He claimed us for Himself, and we rose again to a selfless life in Him : ζῶ δὲ
οὐκέτι ἐγώ, ζῇ δὲ ἐν ἐμοὶ Χριστός.

We act a lie whenever we make our Ego instead
of His Ego the centre. If He is our centre and our
goal, then be sure our Ego will begin to live, because
it is 'grounded' and rooted in His. Any trouble
and anxiety that leads you out of self to the Infinite
Ego, that makes you feel helpless and lonely and in
need of a Human Helper and a Human Comforter,
thank God for it. He is teaching you to cast yourself upon One who is perfectly human because
perfectly divine. He is teaching you that you are
not your own ; that long, long ago yourself died :
εἰ οὖν συνηγέρθητε τῷ Χριστῷ, τὰ ἄνω ζητεῖτε.

Thus we are led to understand something of the
meaning of our Christian names—to see that they
are living pledges to us, whatever we do, wherever we
go—that Christ's name is called upon us—that when
tiny little children we were brought home to the
Great Ego in whom alone our Ego can ever find
satisfaction—to feel that we are His and He is ours.

To J. L. D.

Christ's College, Cambridge : October 9, 1893.

The step which you contemplate taking is one
with far-reaching issues—reaching away through time
and beyond it. I advise you to try and gain a general
idea of the meaning of the first half of St. Paul's

second letter to the Corinthian Church—to try and
enter into its general spirit. Few things will humble
you more : you will see something of the unspeakable
dignity of the office of him who represents God to
his fellow-men, and of the tremendous enthusiasm and
love which a man must have if he would be the
minister that St. Paul would have him be. I do not
know what St. Paul means when he says that we are
ambassadors on behalf of Christ : but the more I
think of what the words seem to mean, the more I
am startled at the awful responsibility that we have
laid upon us. To represent Christ, to treat with men,
to attempt to arrange—if one may so speak—terms,
to use all our powers in performing the work of the
embassy—this at least is involved in the words.
What strikes me so much in the letter is the manner
in which St. Paul literally loves the Church ; how he
longs to communicate his own enthusiasm to it ; how
he would die, almost does die, himself to bring life to
them. All his hopes are bound up with theirs—his
salvation with their salvation. He seems to 'fail
from out his blood, and grow incorporate ' into them.
We are called to the same office as St. Paul, we have
the same power working in us as he had working in
him : we too shall have success in so far as we love
—as we identify ourselves with those whom God has
given us to take care of. The more we are disciplined and yet enthusiastic, the more capable shall we
be of love—of getting out of self—of working our
way into others—of representing the Christ to them—
of understanding and making allowances for them—
of seeing them in the ideal, the only real, light in

which God sees them—seeing them in the Christ, in whom we live—mind that, with all your intellectual training, you don't forget the other. Now is the time to learn, to force yourself to learn, to pray—to pray not for a few minutes at a time, but to pray for an hour at a time—to get alone with yourself—to get alone with your Maker. We shall not have to talk so much to others if we pray more for them. We talk and we do not influence, or we influence only for a time, because our lives are not more prayer-full.

To J. L. D.

Aldeburgh House, Blackheath, S.E.;
December 16, 1893.

I cannot help thinking of you both at this time. It means so much to you both—more than either of you dreams that it means. The issues of your Ordination day are very far reaching indeed. They stretch away and beyond this world in which we now are. The rush of school work and of preparation for examination has probably not left you as much time as you could have wished for thinking over what it all means. I hope you will have more time after the service is over. But you may be comforted in the thought that the last few years have been a definite preparation for your life-work. Though you must regret, as you never regretted before, misuse of time and powers in the past, yet you have had an education which has in some degree prepared you for this time, an education for which you may thank our common Master. But this thought by itself would be but a small comfort. For you must feel, if you are the man I take you for, how unworthy you are to be what you are called to be. Now there are two ways of dealing with this feeling. You may say, 'I am not called to be an absolute saint; but I will try to reach a fairly high standard;' or you may say, 'Yes, I am called to be an absolute saint. I will not lower my ideal. I will comfort myself with that single word "called." If He has called me, He will do in me and for me what He wills.' This second way is the true way of dealing with feelings of unworthiness and unfitness. You and I are utterly unfit. But we are both called—called from our mother's womb—called to be saints and to be ministers. He who called us will help us. With man the call seems quixotic, impossible; with Him all things are possible. At times when the call is loudest we can but reply, 'Ah! Lord, I am but a little child.' We are intensely conscious of feebleness and, what is worse, of treachery and meanness within; we half love what we are called upon to denounce; we play with the sin we are to teach men to abhor. Yet the call is sure, is definite, is perpetual, and again and again you will in all probability find what a help it is to look back to that day in which the call took formal shape. You have that as a definite fact to rest upon, to reprove, to encourage, to urge to renewed effort, to force you to be true and energetic. One thing you must learn to do. Whatever you leave undone you must not leave this undone. Your work will be stunted and half developed unless you attend to it. You must force yourself to be alone and to pray. Do make a point of this. You may be eloquent and attractive in your life, but your real effectiveness depends on your communion with the eternal world. You will easily find excuses. Work is so pressing, and work is necessary. Other engagements take time. You are tired. You want to go to bed. You go to bed late and want to get up late. So simple prayer and devotion are crowded out. And yet, T——, the necessity is paramount, is inexorable. If you and I are ever to be of any good, if we are to be a blessing, not a curse, to those with whom we are connected, we must enter into ourselves, we must be alone with the only source of unselfishness. If we are of use to others, it will chiefly be because we are simple, pure, unselfish. If we are to be simple, pure, unselfish, it will not be by reading books or talking or working primarily, it will be by coming in continual contact with simplicity, purity, unselfishness. Heaven is the possibility of fresh acts of self-sacrifice, of a fuller life of unselfishness. You are a man and a minister in so far as you are unselfish. You cannot learn unselfishness save from the one Source. Definite habits of real devotion—these we must make and keep to and renew and increase. Then we shall gradually find that we are less dependent on self—that even in the busiest scenes we dare not act on our own responsibility—that, be the act ever so small and trifling, when we are in difficulty we shall naturally, inevitably, spontaneously turn to that place whence help alone can come. But it is a wonderful help again and again to feel that we have been

H

alone with Him, that we are not working on our own responsibility, that He is the ' Living Will ' that rises and flows ' through our deeds and makes them pure.'

To F. S. H.

Aldeburgh House, Blackheath : December 16, 1893

Sometimes when I look round and see how some men, some who are infinitely nobler and better than I am, some who have taught me more than they know, and of whom I am utterly unworthy : sometimes when I see these men struggling to find the Truth, unable definitely to receive the facts of the Christian revelation, to whom Christmas brings an uncertain message at best—oh! I feel unutterably contemptible. Why should I see truth, as I believe, and why should they not ? Why am I given an advanced book in God's great school and they are kept back ? And yet they are immeasurably better than I am, and some have better intellectual power also. I know that I hold that lesson book in trust for them, that as I learn I must live out the truth, and teach as well as learn from them. But why was I entrusted with truth ? and why cannot I communicate it ? Why can I love a man almost better than myself, and yet be unable to make him see the Light that is blinding my eyes ? These are questions which you cannot answer and which I cannot answer. The answer is ' behind the veil.' But such unsolved problems do stir me up from my natural laziness, and make me try to develop all my faculties in due proportion in the service of Him who has revealed Himself to me, and who has called me to be His witness and servant. . . . Gradually we shall learn what the service of the intellect means—how vile a heresy it is to suppose that the mind is not to be trained in His school—how unguided spiritual power may be a curse to a man and the community in which he lives. . . .

If you take my advice you will try to get a certain amount of time alone with yourself. I think when we are alone we sometimes see things a little bit more simply, more as they are. Sometimes when we are with others, especially when we are talking to others on religious subjects, we persuade ourselves that we believe more than we do. We talk a great deal, we get enthusiastic, we speak of religious emotions and experiences. This is, perhaps, sometimes good. But when we are alone we just see how much we really believe, how much is mere enthusiasm excited at the moment. We get face to face with Him and our heat and passion go, and what is really permanent remains. We begin to recognise how very little love we have, how very little real pleasure in that which is alone of lasting importance. Then we see how poor and hollow and unloving we are ; then, I think, we also begin to see that this poverty, this hollowness, this unloving void can only be filled by Him who fills all in all. To get alone—to dare to be alone—with God, this, I am persuaded, is one of the best ways of doing anything in the world. It is possible to be constantly speaking of Him, to glow with enthusiasm as we talk about Him to others, and yet to be half-conscious that we dare not quietly face

Him alone. This is my own experience, and I do not doubt that, though you are better than I am, it is yours as well. If we are ever to be or to do anything ; if we are ever to be full of deep, permanent, rational enthusiasm, we must *know* God. If we are ever to know each other we must know Him first. Therefore it is that I want you to dare to be alone and to think. I believe that we do most for those whom God has begun to teach us to love, not by constantly thinking of their goodness, their grace, their simplicity, but by never thinking of them apart from God, by always connecting their beauty and purity with a higher Beauty and a higher Purity by seeing them in God, by seeing God in them. Let us learn to make every thought of admiration and love a kind of prayer of intercession and thanksgiving. Thus human love will correct itself with, and find its root in, Divine love. But this we can only do if we are willing to be alone with Him.

It is a grand thing to think that we are both in the same great school, that we both have the same great Master, and that our discipline is not bounded by this life.

To D. D. R.

8 Alexandra Gardens, Ventnor : Jan. 2, 1894.

While holding as firmly and unreservedly to the belief that a revelation is a possibility that has actually been realised, I am becoming more aware of the partial and limited view which any single individual can have of the significance of such a revelation ; and with this conviction comes a desire not to hinder by any words or prejudices of mine the education of one to whom I owe more than I at present know. Yet, as I believe that no individual life is beyond the wise ordering of a Divine economy, I am sure that he must have lessons to learn from me as well as I to learn from him. Hence I dare not refrain from suggesting to him—often in answer to questions that he puts to me—sides of truth which, as I believe, I have been allowed to apprehend. The knowledge of truth (in however small a degree) is a trust that we hold for the sake of others. What I fear for him and for you— for you even more than for him—is not that you will form wrong opinions on religious or ethical subjects, but that you will lack that moral earnestness that forces a man, whether he will or not, to look the facts of life in the face, that deadly earnestness that refuses to allow us to contemplate creeds as works of art, but forces us to ask whether these things be so. Life as a whole must be faced. What has induced men to believe this and that tenet? Why have men craved for a knowledge of an unseen Being? Why have systems of priestcraft arisen? How is it that those who most revolt against such systems are slaves to other systems bearing different names, but in substance the same? Is there a Deliverer? Is there a unity beneath all this confusion? Can man know such a unity if there be one? Can such a unity be revealed? Has it been revealed? Why do men think it has been revealed if it has not? While I am slow to force upon those whom I most respect and love lessons which I believe that I have slowly learnt in a school in which perhaps they have not been, and never will be, educated, yet I am sure that I cannot be wrong in praying for them and in urging them to be increasingly earnest in the search for and the practice of truth. You are a man in so far as you live. You live in so far as you are self-sacrificing. You are self-sacrificing in so far as you unswervingly practise the truth you know and follow after that which you do not yet apprehend. And I am sure, if there be a unity beneath our lives, if there be One who is educating us when we are most wayward, we shall eventually be led by, it may be, very different paths to a single goal. Meanwhile each failure to be earnest, each relapse into sentimentality, unmanliness, morbidness, despair, unreality, laziness, passiveness, may itself be a discipline, making us utterly mistrust ourselves, whether at our worst or at our best, and forcing us to inquire whether there be any help elsewhere, any power that can sweep through our lives and force us to be human.

For this reason I would impress on you the necessity of trying to think out your position, of asking yourself how you may be most human and best serve God (if, indeed, you believe that this is possible) and your generation. There are around you social forces making for good. Ought you to be—nay, can you be—isolated? Does isolation give greater strength? Does it enable you to do more or to be better? These questions are not merely suggested by me. They have already suggested themselves in one form or another to you. I am frightened of their not receiving the attention they merit.

To T. H. M.

8 Alexandra Gardens, Ventnor : January 3, 1894.

The fact that you have not all the sympathy and manly help and advice that you could wish for from those around you will, I trust, force you to depend with simpler confidence upon the unchanging Ground of all human sympathy. You will, I hope, take all these experiences without grumbling as a real and necessary stage in your education ; remembering that if you find yourself repining at the distressful circumstances in which you are placed, you may be dishonouring Him who has placed you where you are. I do not, of course, mean that such reflection will make you condone and excuse the lukewarmness of others, but you will grasp the truth that God uses even the sin of this world as an instrument in the education of His people, and that you yourself may have your character formed partly through the faults of others, for whom you are still bound to pray.

This great Christmas festival that is past must be a power to us in the year that is coming on. We must enter into and be penetrated by the Life that has been manifested. For it is life that you and I need. Our own puny individualistic life of morbid self-consciousness and sensibility must be transformed by the fuller Life in which all may have a share ; and thus we shall come to think less of ourselves, our successes, our failures, what others think about us and what others ought to think about us—we shall forget all this because we shall share in the Universal Life, which penetrates through all and which makes men forget themselves and their ills, and be pure, simple, healthy, unselfish. And this life has been realised and men have seen it, and it is still with us to-day. In so far as we share in it we shall become natural, unaffected, human. Nay, more. Because the life there manifested is divine as well as human, we shall realise also with fuller force what it is to be a child of a Father who is in heaven. It is life, not a system, that we need. It is life which is given us when we are adopted as sons ; it is life that we receive when the Source of all life gives us Himself to feed upon ; it is life that Christ bestows upon us when we gradually realise our position as members of a society in which no man can live for himself alone. Life is life in so far as it is unselfish. May He who has called us and given to us all our privileges teach us to live out that which we know and believe !

To F. S. H.

Cambridge : August 4, 1895.

Life will not be the same without having you up here. I am very dependent upon others, and I soon begin to be downcast if I have not some one to help or to be helped by. But happily He who takes away is the same as He who gives, and His great heart of affection understands our manifold and seemingly contradictory needs. Life would be intolerable if we had no one who knew us perfectly, not simply the outside part of our life, but that inside and apparently incommunicable part. Those who are least able to express themselves in words, or who (if they did

express themselves) fear that they would be misunderstood, find in Him an unspeakable consolation.
But I must not look at things from the individualistic
standpoint. No problem can ever be solved until we
have in some measure realised that the Life which
flows through us is larger than our own individual
life. We get morbid, and our reason becomes warped,
when we think of our own future alone. Every
obstacle in our path, every interruption to the course
which we have planned for ourselves, every rough
discipline, tells us that our life and future are not our
own, that they are intimately connected with a larger
life, a greater future. I have been thinking of those
words—so like Jesus Christ to have uttered them—
μὴ μεριμνήσητε. We are always anxious about a
set of circumstances which will soon be upon us—
engagements which we tremble to meet. Jesus Christ
tells us, μὴ μεριμνήσητε. I believe that work in the
present world would be far more free and effective if
we would obey the command. We cannot enter into
life as it comes, because we are living in an imaginary
future. The man of God lives in the present; he
leaves the future to God, μὴ μεριμνήσητε. If God
has conducted us so far, He will not leave us. It is
easy to talk, hard to act. I think we gain the power
to act, we gain the calm peace of God, by compelling
ourselves to remain at certain times in His presence.
Habits of prayer are slowly formed, but when formed
are hard to break. Talking may be a great snare
when it takes the place of prayer—and how easily it
does! It is easier to talk with a man than to pray
for him—in many cases.

To F. S. H.

Clovelly : September 11, 1895.

I am reading 'The Newcomes': have you ever read it? I find it hard to appreciate Thackeray as much as some people do. Occasionally he says some very true things and shows that he is acquainted with human nature in its brighter and darker aspects. But, on the whole, the story of marriage and giving in marriage—selling your daughter for money or a title—the picture of young men who sow their wild oats and then repent and marry innocent ladies and live virtuously and die in the odour of sanctity—on the whole the story does not seem to correspond to the ideals which haunt me, even though I do not act up to them. Surely life is something utterly different from all this. Surely somewhere there is a picture of human life, somewhere in the mind of God Himself, where the young man grows up without any harvest of wild oats, with clear and unselfish ideals, with a longing to make the world purer and diviner than he found it, a picture which is in some measure realised around us to-day. May God deliver us not only from vicious but from selfish thoughts! I believe Thackeray saw something of that picture, but he didn't draw it with the colours I could have wished. There is a solemn text in Ezekiel, which came in the lesson lately, 'The righteousness of the righteous shall not deliver him in the day of his transgression.' Past religious experiences are of little value without present righteousness.

To his cousin G. F.

Clovelly, N. Devon : September 12, 1895.

I am in perhaps the quaintest and one of the loveliest villages in England, just doing nothing, and enjoying the simple life around me. You would like this village, with its one steep, narrow, picturesque street, the great sea far down below, the little stone pier jutting out and helping to form a small harbour. Then on either side of the village are woods reaching down to the cliffs—beautiful woods, where oaks, and in places heather, are glad to grow. St. Paul says in the lesson to-day that the things which are seen are temporal, but the things which are not seen are eternal. And one feels how true are his words— how the trees, woods, flowers fade and die ; how the old sea wears slowly away the cliffs ; how men and their dwellings pass away ; how all these things which are seen are temporal ; and yet the beauty, the love, the joy, the purity, are more permanent than the particular manifestations of them are. The beauty which is manifested in the country around is eternal. The life which is seen in man has a future beyond this world.

As we enter in behind the veil, as we see that life and love which are expressing themselves in objects around us, we are already in the eternal, in that which endures.

It is not, as we are constantly thinking, the things that are *present* which are temporal, and the things that are *future* which are eternal. No : the things which are present have an eternal side to them—the unseen side.

The man who is a slave to the seen has least of the eternal about him : the man who despises not the seen, but who through the seen rises to the unseen, is partaking of eternal life. . . .

To F. S. H.

Cambridge : October 23, 1895.

Let me congratulate you on the way you ran against Yale.[1] I was delighted to read of your 'romping' home !! . . . . It seems to me that every unfulfilled longing is no accidental part of life. The longing, in so far as it is genuinely human, is derived from Him in whose image man is made. When it is hard to see why it is not gratified, yet we may confidently believe that this is part of our training. Is it not a noble work to enter into and, in some measure, bear the burdens of other men's lives, even if they have only imperfect sympathy with ours ? May we not sometimes even learn more in this way— or at least learn different lessons—than if they were so similar to ourselves that they could at once understand us ? I am afraid that you have a hard struggle before you. You must take care not to act upon first impressions, or impulse—not even if those impressions are favourable . . . your best 'pearls' must be used carefully.

[1] In the international athletic sports in U.S.A.

To F. S. H. on his going to a curacy in Liverpool.

Cambridge : October 18, 1896.

In some respects I am glad to hear of your change of plans. I think you will be more in your element working in a poor part of a large town. . . . Our dean has just been preaching on the words ' One soweth, and another reapeth.' It is a help to realise the continuity of work. We enter into the work of many a man who has passed away, and who, while he worked, often despaired and thought that he was achieving nothing. No work is lost. The obscure and petty—these are relative terms. We use them, but we are told on the best authority that there is nothing secret which shall not be made manifest. The consciousness of the continuity and perpetuity of work quiets and calms us ; we need not hurry over anything. When we have left off sowing, others will reap. God give us grace to work, for the night cometh when no man can work. I am so sorry that I have not been able to come up and see you. But we are working in the same field, though it is too large across to see one another !

To C. T. W.

St. Moritz : February 1898.

Two new toboggan runs have been opened : one is a Canadian run on soft snow without turns, short and sweet ; the other is part of the Crista run, an ice

run, which I suppose is quite the finest in the world,
with splendid corners. When it is all made it will
be about a mile in length. . . . In a noisy salon it
is difficult to collect my scattered thoughts. Music
and other atrocities are in full swing ; and as I
seldom use my brain now, the works are rusty. I
wish you could see this country in winter. . . . A
male rival of The Brook has appeared. He is impressed with the dust and dampness of the atmosphere—takes out trays to toboggan on into Italy—
sprinkles water on his bedroom floor, because he
considers a damp atmosphere conducive to sleep.
So far we have not fallen out altogether with one
another ; some of us are on speaking terms. We
only confidentially discuss whether so-and-so has
come here for his mind. We have an archdeacon, a
canon, a curate, two captains ; one Plymouth-brother-
like, who takes most gloomy views about the future
of us, or most of us, including the parsons ; the other
very noisy, who attempted the Canadian toboggan
run which is supposed to be safe for ladies and
children, and swears that he almost broke his neck.
He had an upset and went head foremost into the
snow, and, according to his own account, had to be
dug out. If he had been a heavier man, I understand that he would have broken his neck. As two
accidents have occurred there, it is not absolutely
safe. . . . This place is a splendid pick-me-up. I
am a reformed character—go to bed between 6 and
10.30 P.M. I was detected last night cheating at
cards. But reformation to be effective requires time.
Give up, I say, one bad habit at a time, and then

tackle the next. I have given up early rising as being the most patent of my evil practices.

To J. K.

Christ's College, Cambridge : August 19, 1898.

. . . . I am sure that we have need to learn not only in the school of health but also in the school of sickness. These breaks in life, and the sense of helplessness and weakness which attend them, are not simply periods to be 'got over '—to be made the best of till we can 'start again '—but they have a meaning which we can find, if we only look with the eye of faith. It is strange how, although God sees the whole way in which we ought to go, He leaves us in comparative darkness. We need, I am sure, *revelation*. 'Lord, open the young man's eyes, that he may see.' We shall take the wrong turning if we trust to our ordinary eyes ; we shall find the path if we have the eye of faith to see what God is revealing. . . . And now at this time I need your prayers. I have—and this, I need hardly say, is private—an invitation from the Bishop of —— to come and lecture to theological students, whom he hopes to gather round him. Of course the scheme is rather in the air so far. He has not yet got the men. But he has an attractive power, and he might on a smaller scale do some such work as Vaughan used to do for men who did not go to definite theological colleges. Will you pray for me that I may go if I ought, and not go if I ought not, please ?

> Our wills are ours, we know not how,
> Our wills are ours, to make them Thine.

To J. L. D.

Cliff Dale, Cromer : October 3, 1898.

I do not belong and I never have belonged to any
of the societies or guilds which you mention.   I am
a member of a Church.   For that reason I dare not
join any party.   In fact, I cannot understand what
'parties' have to do with a Church.   The Church by
its very existence is a witness against parties and
divisions.   It will take me more than a lifetime to
learn what it is to be a member of a Church ; and no
one can learn the lesson while he persists in clinging
to a party.   He must be a member not of a *part* but
of a *whole*.   I therefore have no time to waste in
joining a party.

I feel strongly that the various societies and
guilds, based upon *party* life, are eating away the very
life of the Church.   But I am slow in condemning
my neighbour for conscientiously joining any such
society.   He may only be able to see one side of
truth, and it is better—far better—that he should see
that side than nothing at all.

To the mother of his godchild, Margaret Forbes.

April 12, 1899.

It is such a joy to me to be allowed to be her
godparent, and I shall remember her often in my
prayers.   What a wonderful revelation she must be
to you both—making the Heavenly Home a fuller
reality than ever before !   It is through earthly rela-

tionships that we realise the meaning of the unseen world.   I like those lines of Faber :

> All fathers learn their craft from Thee :
> All loves are shadows cast
> By the beautiful eternal hills
> Of Thine unbeginning past.

To his mother.

Rouxville, Orange Free State : July 8, 1899.

It is a strange and somewhat terrible study in religion—this Boer religion.   It seems to have little or no connection with morality.   Kruger seems to have amassed great wealth by doubtful means.   A man comes to him and offers him, say, 8,000*l.* on condition that he may have the right to sell mineral waters. Mrs. Kruger comes in and counts the money ; and if it is right, the concession is granted.   Yet he is religious, very religious.   A short time ago they wanted to fire shells into the low-lying clouds during a time of drought.   The clouds gather, but they will not break.   Firing shells was found to have a good effect in bringing the rain.   But Kruger stopped it because it was wrong to 'fire shells at the Almighty.'   You would think that a little state like this might be an ideal one with its simple scattered population of farmers.   But it is by no means so.   Corruption and injustice are only too prevalent.   At the start off they were unfortunate in their choice of President.   The state was at war with the Basutos at the time when he was elected ; and three months after he was made

I

President he had to be deposed, because he was discovered selling arms to the Basutos.

The Dutch don't treat the natives as well as we do. Yet in some respects their laws are wise. A native may not live in the Free State without doing some definite work, unless he pays a tax of 5s. a month : this is, I think, a wise rule.

We had two very nice services last Sunday at the English church ; I preach twice to-morrow.

To C. T. W.

Durban : July 1899.

I write to congratulate you most heartily on your First Class. . . . I believe you will find in a year's time that whatever your work may be, contact with others—the necessity of influencing and guiding them—will be a tremendous help to you in your own life. . . .

Good man ! I am delighted to think that you may see the Bishop of Durham. Prophets' eyes are needed out here to catch the glory which must be slowly—so slowly—gaining on the shade. There is so much materialism, so little refinement and spirituality.

I had a grand voyage : only three people rescued from drowning before I got on board, and two stowaways after we left Madeira, and two or three days of rough weather. I enjoyed it. . . .

I had afternoon tea, or rather coffee, with Uncle Paul. He is a strong, fine old man. He was sitting puffing away at his large pipe. It was after a long day's work in the secret Volksraad. He was tired.

' It is hard work,' he said, ' for the head.' The State attorney, a young Christ's man, explained to him that ' we were both at the same school in England.' Kruger was eloquent on the subject of the Petition. He told me that some of the 21,000 had died three years before they signed it, and some had signed it owing to a bottle of whisky. ' And I want you to let that be known in England ' (I know anything said to you will circulate—by experience). He said, did the subtle old man, that he wanted to do what was right and fair irrespective of nationality.

This Transvaal question is complicated. I thought it easy at first. But now I can see no moral grounds of any sort for a war with the Boers, in spite of their iniquities. There is a great deal to be said on their side, and much iniquity concealed under such specious phrases as ' Imperialism,' ' Supremacy of Great Britain in South Africa.' I cannot see that we have a real cause for war, but it is a big question with many sides. If England goes to war and wins, she will have her work cut out. ' Can she afford,' said the Attorney of the Transvaal to me, ' to have a second Ireland at the distance of some 5,000 or 6,000 miles from home ? What if she had war in India ? '

To W. A. B.

Lucknow Lodge, Berea, Durban : August 22, 1899.

I thank my God in my prayers on your behalf for His goodness in granting you His best gift—a human soul to love and to inspire. Together you will be able to know and love Him better than either of you could alone. You cannot make your love too sacred ; as you know God you will learn to know one another.

We are inclined to think that we know all that love means. The truth is, we are only beginners. Thank God that we are in the school, although only in one of the lowest forms. He will teach us, as years go by, to sanctify ourselves for the sake of another. We have not learned to love until we are living the highest possible life, in order that the object of our affection may become a saint. God is giving you a present, the value of which you see in part now, you will realise fully hereafter. You must wrestle with God for her and for yourself. If you are true to the highest, both of you will rise together and see God. If you are not, she may not be able to mount alone.

I am filled with joy and hope as I think of you both. I believe that you will live for God more completely now than ever before, and that you will be a fuller blessing to your people. You have my prayers. I want you to make your ideals higher and higher. Then, when you have gained one height, you will find that what you took for the summit from the plain was not really so : there were further peaks beyond.

It is the beginning of an endless life. If God Himself be the centre of all, the nearer we are to Him, the nearer we are to one another. I *am* glad that your wife is one who shares in your ideals, who lives for the highest. What a life in store for you here ! And there—

Before the judgment seat,
Though changed and glorified each face,
Not unremembered you will meet
For endless ages to embrace.

You will be nearer the centre then, and nearer to one another.

May God Himself bless you, dear old fellow! Forgive this poor attempt at a letter. I share in your joy, although I am not actually with you. I never remember any wedding outside my own family which has given me greater pleasure. It was good of you to ask me to be present—very good.

B——, I *am* glad. You must thank God and ask Him to tell you what it all means, and for her sake live as good a life as you possibly can.

With best love I am your friend,

FORBES.

To a Friend after hearing of his intended ordination.

Durban : August 1899.

Your ordination will be like my own over again. It is unutterably good of God . . . to put it into your heart to live the life which I had prayed might be yours. Μειζοτέραν τούτων οὐκ ἔχω χάριν, ἵνα ἀκούω τὰ ἐμὰ τέκνα ἐν τῇ ἀληθείᾳ περιπατοῦντα . . .

. . . If your temptations are great it is because your nature is rich and noble ; and when it is disciplined you will have tremendous power. I shall not be content until your every thought is led captive to ' the obedience of the Christ.' You are born to be a saint, and you will be wretched until you are one. You are not the kind of man who can do things by halves.

I think I have told you of my father's words spoken during his last illness : ' If I had a thousand

lives, I would give them all—all to the ministry.'
You will not regret your decision. If angels could
envy, how they would envy us our splendid chance
—to be able, in a world where everything unseen
must be taken on sheer faith, in a world where the
contest between the flesh and the spirit is being
decided for the universe, not only to win the battle
ourselves but also to win it for others ! To help a
brother up the mountain while you yourself are only
just able to keep your foothold, to struggle through
the mist together—that surely is better than to stand
at the summit and beckon. You will have a hard
time of it, I know ; and I would like to make it
smoother and to 'let you down' easier ; but I am
sure that God, who loves you even more than I do,
and has absolute wisdom, will not tax you beyond
your strength. . . . I'll pray for you, like the widow
in the parable, and I have immense belief in prayer.
. . . You remember what was said of Maurice, ' He
always impressed me as a man who was naturally
weak in his will ; but an iron will seemed to work
through him.' That Will can work through you and
transform you, but for God's sake don't trust to your
own will. . . .

If you are ordained it will be because there is one
who in St. Paul's words—ὁ ἀφορίσας με ἐκ κοιλίας
μητρός μου—was separating you from birth and
educating you with a view to the Gospel of Christ. . . .

> Tasks in hours of insight willed
> Can be through hours of gloom fulfilled.[1]

[1] Matthew Arnold, *Morality*.

To his mother.

Estcourt, Natal: August 18, 1899.

General Gordon came to Kokstad on his way to
Basutoland.   When he arrived he went to the Royal
Hotel, ordered a room, threw open the window, and
spent two hours in prayer and meditation.   The
next day was Sunday.   He asked Mr. Adkin what
was being done for 1,000 Cape Mounted Infantry
then stationed there, and when he learnt that nothing
was being done for their spiritual food, he burst into
tears.   On Monday morning the first telegram which
he sent off to the Cape Government was a request
that a chaplain should be appointed.   Mr. Adkin
was appointed and remained chaplain until the force
was disbanded.   General Gordon went on to Basutoland, and had wonderful power over the natives.
He told them that no force would be brought against
them ;   he himself was without weapons.   He was
settling the country, when news came to him that
the Cape Government was, contrary to stipulation,
sending an armed force against them ;   so he left the
country in twenty-four hours.

Cecil Rhodes was once at Kokstad.   When he
was near the place, he lay down on the hillside and
exclaimed : 'Oh, how I wish they would let me
alone—let me stay here !'   However, he had to go
down to be fêted.   He was listless, and bored by the
banquet, until the present mayor began to attack him
violently in his speech, and to complain about the
Cape Government, and to express a desire that Natal
would take them over.   Then Rhodes woke up with

a vengeance and gave them a great speech. Ixopo
is where Rhodes started out in South Africa. His
name still figures on the magistrates' books—fined
10*l.* for selling a gun to a native.

*To his cousin, J. C. H., on the occasion of the death
of his brother.*

December 7, 1899.

You know, without my saying it, that you have
my deep sympathy and prayers at this time. . . .
We dare not and cannot sorrow as do others who
have no certain hope. Our sorrow is of another
kind. For I am quite sure that

In His vast world above,
A world of broader love,
God hath some grand employment for His son.[1]

How real it all makes that other world, to have our
own brothers there! It makes it in a deeper sense
our home.

To the mother of his godchild, Margaret Forbes.

Doré House, St. Leonards : January 10, 1900.

I am so glad to feel that my little godchild will
have real training. I don't know how far I received
such a training myself at an early age . . . I came
towards the end of a large family. The only permanent instruction which I can remember imparted
to me by my nursery maid was a caution not to look

[1] Faber, *The Old Labourer.*

behind me when I passed people in the street, enforced by the biblical precept, 'Remember Lot's wife.' I know what a fascination I had to look behind, accompanied by a terrible dread of the consequences.

I have always felt that Faber's 'God of my Childhood' describes the normal and true development of a child's life. I am sure that, although the gravity of sin should be early recognised, greater stress should be laid upon the Fatherhood and kindness of God. I was noticing to-day, when reading the second lesson, how Westcott and Hort have placed the clause in the Lord's Prayer which speaks of the Fatherhood of God in a line by itself as a heading to the whole prayer, putting a colon after the clause, and beginning the first petition with a capital letter. The prayer begins with 'Fatherhood' and ends with a reference to 'Sinfulness.' I think this fact is significant. We may not all be intended to come to know religious truth in that order. But I think we are intended, when we do know it, to lay even more stress on the Fatherhood of God than on our own imperfections. It is a wonderful and terrible thing to watch the development of a human spirit. We can understand so little about any life, even when it is near and dear to us. But I am not sure that we cannot learn more about others than we can about ourselves. I never think it is profitable to study oneself too closely! I never could meditate with any profit on my sins. But there, I dare say, I differ from many others.

Well, I hope that the hair of my godchild is

growing, and that she has now more than her god-father. His is coming to an untimely end.

To F. S. H., who had recently become a chaplain in the Navy.

St. Leonards : January 11, 1900.

I am thinking of you in your new, difficult, and interesting life, and wondering how you like it. Or, rather, I am sure that you like it in its main features. There are in every life drawbacks and discourage-ments, for we live by faith and not by sight, and faith must be perfected in the midst of perplexities and contradictions. The mists are useful. It would not do to have brilliant sunshine all the time. For in that case, where would faith come in ? Steering towards our port in the fog means trusting the Pilot. ' Mercifully grant that we, which know Thee now by faith, may after this life have the fruition of Thy glorious Godhead.' I suppose that none of us fully knows what this prayer means. I think that there will be more need of faith hereafter than we usually think. Can we ever apprehend the Father or the Son without faith ? The deepest truths are grasped by faith not sight. The man who has learned to exercise faith here will have fuller scope for his faith hereafter. What a shock to wake up in the next world and to find that the riddles of life still need faith for their solution ! Yet I imagine that it will be so. Only faith will be able to go deeper than here. The faith perfected in the mists of life will, in the sunshine of eternity, see deeper into the meaning of events. I wish I had more faith. Not sudden flights of faith annihilating time and space and rising up to the throne of heaven. But I wish I could ground all my actions on faith, and regularly see the invisible and live as one who could see always and everywhere the Unseen. We are schooled in different ways. We cannot attain to perfection in a night. As we advance in the Christian life progress seems slower. In some sense it is so. It is easier to cast off a number of definite bad habits clearly inconsistent with the ideal just at first, than to perfect self-sacrifice, humility, and self-discipline. But we are advancing, though we know it not. If the engines are always kept working, we shall reach our goal !

To C. N. W., who had recently been ordained.

St. Leonards-on-Sea : January 12, 1900.

You must remember how much your future efficiency is dependent upon a judicious use of your strength during the next two or three years. I am sure you are right in looking back upon your life and tracing in its developments a higher than human guidance. It is a helpful thing to trace now and anon God's hand in our individual life. It brings Him nearer to us, and it is an awful thought that He is actually working within us. It makes us trust Him for time to come even when the prospect is gloomy. I think that we do well to spend some time in trying to interpret details of our past life. As years go on, we should have such a firm faith founded on the rock of experience that we will not be lightly shaken. Peace should be a characteristic of our life—the joy and peace which come from a certainty that there is a Purpose in all events. The sense that God has been with us in the past is a help in interpreting the history of our nation. Even our troubles are a proof that He is disciplining us. For the service of Intercession, which my brother uses in Westminster Abbey at the time of this war, the opening sentence is ' The Lord our God be with us,' and the answer is, ' As He was with our fathers.'

The College is getting on well. You must come up and see me this year, while you still know a number of men. I have now a little evening service —compline—in my rooms at 10 o'clock ; Masterman asked me to have it. He asked men to come, and they asked others. I purposely refrained from asking any one. We are sometimes a goodly number. I think it is helpful to those who come. It is, I know, to me. We have a hymn when we have sufficient musical talent !

To G. J. C.

Christ's College, Cambridge : 1900.

Gwatkin has exploded Anthony, ' who never existed.' But for all that I think Anthony is much like Adam and Eve. The originals may ' never have existed.' Yet their story belongs to all time. And there will be Anthonies and Adams and Eves to the end of time. It comforts me to feel that that which makes for evil is not my true self, but a wretched, cunning animal existence independent of me, exist-

ing before I came into being, although capable of
appealing to me—a serpent.

I am half glad and half sorry to hear of your
harmonium.   Public worship is a terribly difficult
thing, and it is well at times that we should realise
its difficulties, and have it stripped bare of many
helpful accessories.   Yet worship in a village church
impresses me.   As in a college chapel, I realise
then the continuity of the race.   An old church
tells me of generations of men who lived my life,
to whom the present was everything, and the dead
almost nothing, who never could seriously believe
that some day the world would whirl and follow
the sun without them.   It tells me more than
most things of what St. Paul means when he said
that we were all making one perfect man.   And I
am humbled and thankful to know that I in my
generation can do something towards the Christ 'that
is to be.'

Read the Old Testament itself.   Nothing will
atone for lack of knowledge of the Bible.   Robertson
Smith's and Adam Smith's books (especially the
latter's) on the Old Testament Prophets ought to
prove useful. . . . When I call a man by his Christian
name, I usually make it a rule to pray for him.
I shall do so in your case.   I will try to pray every
day.   I wonder whether you would sometimes pray
for me : I believe immensely in the power of prayer.
It is the greatest favour I can ask of you, and I know
I have no right to prefer the request ; but it would
be kind of you if you could occasionally.   One needs
all the help one can get in this strange life up here.

Now I will end.   I have written you a strange,
unreserved letter.   Forgive me.   How I wish this
dreadful war was at an end !   U——'s going was a
blow to me ; but I am sure he did the right thing.
I admire and love that man. . . .

To G. J. C.

Castleton, Swanage : 1900.

. . . You will not have misinterpreted my silence.
I could not answer your letter until I had secured a
time for quiet thought and for prayer.   When I try
to write, I feel the uselessness of words.   I am doing
better when I am praying for you than when I am
writing to you.   Yet I must write. . . . It is strange
that God should have made us thus.   To those whom
He honours most He gives largest capacity for love,
and therefore largest capacity for suffering.   It is
still more strange that we would not wish to be without the love in spite of the agony which it brings.
It must be because

> All loves are shadows cast
> By the beautiful eternal hills
> Of Thine unbeginning past.

I feel this truth 'in seasons of calm weather.'   But
at other times I ask myself, I ask God, angrily,
Why should some men have no obstacle to their
love ?   Why should another suffer more than any one
can tell—more than, it sometimes seems to me, can
ever be requited ?   I cannot answer the question.
But I often think of the great unsatisfied heart of
God, and then I think of this poor unsatisfied heart

made in His image, and I feel that He understands me, and that I understand Him better than I used to do, before this terrible hunger of love began.

I pray God that He will deal tenderly with you, G——, and I am sure that He will. It cuts me to the heart to think of your suffering, and I would stop it this moment if I could. So would God—for He loves you more than I do—unless it were the best thing for you. It is written of the Son of man, ἔμαθεν ἀφ᾽ ὧν ἔπαθεν. May the same words be true of you and of me! God bless you and give you Light and Peace!

> Peace is something more than joy,
> Even the joys above;
> For peace, of all created things,
> Is likest Him we love.

This letter may appear cold to you. It is not I feel more deeply than I write. . . . Some day, if you care to hear, I will tell you something about my own imperfect life. I can't write it down. Later the day will dawn. But God sends the darkness that we may learn to trust Him. I have never yet found Him to fail. We cannot trust Him too much.

To the mother of a friend, after having been present at his funeral.

Cambridge : April 22, 1900.

I feel I must write and tell you how grateful I am to you for your kindness in allowing me to be present on Thursday. Whenever I think of your son who has passed away, that text comes into my mind : 'Blessed are the pure in heart, for they shall see God.' He was pure in heart, and I cannot think of him as lifeless, but as actually seeing God. . . . I am thankful to have been allowed to be his friend. I shall never forget him ; his life remains a source of strength and inspiration to me. It comforts me now to know that he is sinking deeper and deeper into the peace of God, which passeth all understanding. You were talking to me about W——; I could not say all that I wished to say. . . . I am very, very slow to suggest ordination to a man. I realise the responsibility of doing so, but there is no man whom I desire to see ordained more than W——; he has been to me more help than I can possibly say. I dare not try to tell you all that he has done for me, because you would think I was exaggerating. I cannot help feeling that, if he helps me so much, he might help others also, and that, if he were ordained, he would have singular opportunities for rendering such help. But I do not press him in the matter, because I might do wrong ; but I pray again and again that, if God wishes him to be ordained, He will make His purpose clear, and I am quite sure that He will not leave us in the dark.

To C. T. W.

Cambridge : July 1900.

I was delighted to read in the paper yesterday of your election to a fellowship. . . . The life will be a harder one than that of an ordinary parish clergy-man ; it will be easier to lose sight of ideals. But the importance of the work is in proportion to its difficulty. Blessed is the man who finds his work, and does it ; and you will be blessed. . . .

You should read St. Patrick's 'Confession,' a genuine work of my distinguished countryman. It is full of humility and zeal. I give you a quotation : 'After I had come to Ireland I used daily to feed cattle, and I often prayed during the day. More and more did the love of God and the fear of Him increase, and faith became stronger and the spirit was moved ; so that in one day I said as many as a hundred prayers, and in the night nearly the same. . . . And there was no sluggishness in me, as I now see there is, for at that time the spirit was fervent within me.' Pathetic—that last part. He might have been living at Cambridge ! But I hope better things for you.

To C. T. W.

Thirlmere : September 1900.

My thoughts are with you now—and my prayers. 'He had seven stars—in His right hand,' was the thought which comforted me at my own ordination, when I felt, as seldom before, my own hollowness and incapacity. We can shed light—we are safe—because we are 'in His right hand.' 'The eternal God is our refuge, and underneath are the everlasting arms.' We can never go beyond His love and care. In moments of perplexity and uncertainty, although we cannot feel His presence, He is there. 'In His right hand.' 'They that turn many to righteousness shall shine as the stars for ever and ever.'

K

May God give you the power to love and the power to pray! Much prayer and much love are needed for a successful ministry. Good-bye, and God bless you and make you a true and faithful pastor! Remember St. Paul's words : ἡ δύναμις ἐν ἀσθενείᾳ τελεῖται. ἥδιστα οὖν μᾶλλον καυχήσομαι ἐν ταῖς ἀσθενείαις, ἵνα ἐπισκηνώσῃ ἐπ' ἐμὲ ἡ δύναμις τοῦ Χριστοῦ· ὅταν γὰρ ἀσθενῶ, τότε δυνατός εἰμι.

To W. D. H.

Dale Head Post Office, Thirlmere: September 20, 1900.

My thoughts and my prayers are with you at this time. I remember how at my own ordination, when I felt as never before my own utter weakness and incapacity, the thoughts in the first chapter of the Revelation, of Christian ministers as stars in His right hand' comforted and supported me. In His right hand—with His power we can do all things. As the lesson for to-day says, ἡ δύναμις ἐν ἀσθενείᾳ τελεῖται, strength is perfected in weakness. ὅταν ἀσθενῶ, τότε δυνατός εἰμι.

You will feel more, as years go on, the greatness of the task which you are undertaking—the over-whelming responsibility— the dread lest through any carelessness on your part one of the least of the sheep may be lost. But you will also feel more and more that you are 'in His right hand.' And if the eternal God is your refuge and underneath are the everlasting arms, you need not fear what the devil or man can do unto you. I pray that God may be with you and give you the spirit of prayer and the spirit of love

Your ministry will only be effective if you pray much and love much. And if you make mistakes, yet if you love much your sins will be forgiven.

To his brother, a doctor in South Africa.

September 1900.

When I feel what the grace of God has done for my life, what it is doing, what it will do, I can despair of no one else. I am filled with wonder and amazement and thanksgivings and hopes. I am sometimes so thankful that I still live, that in a world of light and dark shadows I can show my faith in God, before the other world dawns with its full day and unclouded brightness—and most of all that I can here and now pray for those whom He has taught me to love. I cannot conceive this world without prayer. It is worth while making any efforts, however desperate, to learn to pray. When the Day dawns, how wonderful it will be to look back and trace the path through which He has led us in the Twilight!

To F. J. C.

Christ's College, Cambridge : 1900.

The more He tries you by His silence, the greater to my mind is the proof that He believes in you. He knows you will come through. He has great work for you to do, and therefore you need a strong, perfected faith, and He is trying to give you it.

I am so sorry at what you tell me about prayer. But do go on. When things are at their darkest, light comes. After all God knows how much you can bear, and He will not, if you will only persevere, allow you to be utterly confounded. Don't be in the least discouraged at your inability to concentrate your attention. Even a man who had lived in the presence of God for years has told us that

> The world that looks so dull all day
> Glows bright on me at prayer,
> And plans that ask no thought but these,
> Wake up and meet me there.
> My very flesh has restless fits ;
> My changeful limbs conspire
> With all these phantoms of the mind
> My inner self to tire.

Do you expect to fare better, when you are exercising faculties which have been for long more or less dormant ? The same man goes on to say—and I think it is a comforting truth—that God sees further than we do, sees what we mean :

> These surface troubles come and go,
> Like rufflings of the sea ;
> The deeper depth is out of reach
> To all, my God, but Thee.

Even if your conscience condemns you, remember that God is greater than your conscience. He sees that you *want* to pray, and the battle is half won when there is even the want. I like these old words of the hymn :

> Satan trembles when he sees
> The weakest saint upon his knees,

even if he can't collect his thoughts. I find it

usually easier to pray for others than for myself. I believe in beginning by praying for what is easiest. I don't kneel down. I find it more possible to concentrate my attention when I am walking about or sitting down. And I tell God what I know about a man, and how I want him to live a better life. Sometimes I seem to struggle for him as though for very life. I go on and on and on—sometimes repeating the same request. I try to copy the poor widow who wearied out the dishonest judge. I am not distressed when my thoughts wander. I know that they will always wander without God's help. The distress occasioned by wandering thoughts, and the attempt to trace the stages by which they wandered, I regard as temptations of the devil. . . . I go back as calmly as possible to the matter in hand.

Excuse my 'egoism.' I put it in the first person, because I believe my own experience will help you more than rules derived from the experience of others.

Suppose you spend half an hour in this way, and only really pray for three or four minutes, your efforts will be more than rewarded. You will have done more than you know for the person for whom you have prayed. And the next half-hour you will find that you can concentrate your attention for a minute or two longer. Don't think too much about yourself when you pray. You must lose your soul if you would save it.

There is probably some one thing or some one person easier than others for you to pray for. Begin with that.

I never try, as some people do, to classify and

enter into details about my sins. I bring the whole
contradictory, weary, and unintelligible mass of them
to God, and leave them with Him. I am quite sure
I shall never do better without Him. But I know
that He believes in me, and will help me in spite of
myself. He believes in you too, dear old fellow!
May God bless you for your kindness to me! Write
me just a short note to tell me that you don't despise
me in spite of what must seem to you rather unintelligible and ridiculous confessions.

I can't help it. And if you can bring yourself to
do it, call me too by my Christian name.

To the same.

Christ's College, Cambridge: September 28, 1900.

I feel more and more the necessity of being alone
occasionally for some time—to get time enough to
pray. I think my supreme desire is to be a man of
prayer. You must help me to accomplish the desire :
' Gutta cavat lapidem non vi, sed sæpe cadendo.'

So it is with prayer. As the stone gets worn
away, not by the force of the drop of water but by its
constant trickling, so prayer often renewed must at
length attain its end. It is a wonderful privilege to
be able to state all one's wishes and hopes for others
in prayer —to know that there can be there no possibility of misunderstanding—to tell to God the in-
comprehensible depth of one's love, and to feel that
He knows what it means, because He Himself is love.
It is glorious to be made in His image, and to be sure
that all one's highest yearnings are a reflection—
however broken, partial, and unsightly—of His own

marvellous life. We have indeed cause to be grateful for our 'creation.' I often look at the poor dumb creatures, and thank God that He has given me such full powers of love, which they cannot understand : for I would rather have the pains of love than any other pleasure.

To F. S. H., a chaplain in the Navy.

Cambridge : November 4, 1900.

I ought to have written before this. The fact that I did not answer at once is partly accounted for by my having a good deal of work to do, and partly by physical weakness. I have not been very well this term. It is cruel of you to suspect me of having forgotten all about you. I am not that sort. I owe too much to you in the past ever to forget you. I don't think that you really suspected me of inconstancy. I am so sorry that you are sometimes lonely and very miserable. I feel at times weak, physically weak. I think that at such times one can lean back, as it were, on the Divine arms. He understands our weakness and weariness. He knows what loneliness and sadness mean. And He is not extreme to mark what we do amiss. He knows that we are but flesh. And He 'dwells not in the light alone, but in the darkness and the light.' Even when the darkness hides Him and we cannot find where He is, we can, as it were, reach out our hands to Him, and we are safe. God has much to teach us while we are teaching others. And life is not exactly the same as we thought at the beginning. He teaches us by unex-

pected experiences. But the comfort is that He never
changes ; we may be weary, but He never slumbers
nor sleeps. Sometimes we feel very fit and capable.
Then is the time to pray and to rise to the heights.
Later, when we are incapable, although it is hard to
rise, we need not fall. When the mist clears we can
go on again, and it may be that we shall find that
even in the mist we had gone further than we
thought. The deep snow and the long dark rainy
days are necessary for the perfecting of the fruit,
as well as the sunshine. And we do need sunshine.
I feel more and more grateful and thankful to God
for His goodness. He has been so good to me, and
I don't deserve it. And I think that if you look
back and look forward you will feel more and more
His marvellous sympathy and affection. I am glad
you have been reading Robertson's Life. Though he
may have been almost morbid at times, he was a
great man and did a great work. . . . You will find
later that your work has been far more effective than
you expected. Don't try to rush it. You can't help
men much until you know them very well ; and
when you know them you find how utterly different
they are from what you had expected them to be. At
least I do. No two men are alike. Each man that
you come really to know is utterly different from
any man you have ever met or will meet.

To F. J. C.

Christ's College, Cambridge : November 5, 1900.

It is good of you to think of me and above all to
pray for me. I need your prayers—and most of all

when I am run down and unable to pray myself. I can see the mountain top at times : then the mist comes down, and I cannot see the way ; I try to keep where I am, though I may not be able to advance ; and when the mist clears I go on again. Possibly, sometimes, we may be going forward even in the mist, although we seem to be making no progress, or going backward.

> God judges by a light
> Which baffles mortal sight.

I often wish I had more physical strength and was able to do what other men can do ; but I can't. And I have no doubt that all is well—that I am made to do one particular piece of work, and that I have strength enough for that—and thank God for that.

To a brother in South Africa.

December 1900.

It is a marvellous thought that God can reveal Himself to man—even primitive man. In those stories Jehovah is very near to man. He walks in the garden at nightfall. He shuts Noah into the Ark. He comes down to see the city and the tower 'which the children of men builded.' He talks with Moses face to face as a man speaketh to his friend— and a ladder connects heaven and earth, and the angels, instead of using wings, walk up and down the ladder—and, behold, Jehovah stood above it. At any moment you might meet Jehovah Himself. Three men come to see Abraham—and Jehovah has

appeared to him. A man wrestles with Jacob, and
he has seen God face to face. They were right when
they thought of God as very near to man, of man as
capable of reflecting God's likeness. Ye too shall
see heaven opened and the angels of God ascending
and descending upon—the Son of man. It is good
for us as children to read these stories to realise that
heaven is very near to earth. It is good for us as
men to read them again to realise that heaven is even
nearer earth than we thought as children. As I said
before, how marvellous it is that God can reveal
Himself to man and through man, that He has
revealed Himself entirely, ' the perfect man,' as
Maurice says, reflecting the perfect God—God and
man so near one to the other that men can look
upon the Son of man and see God—see Him in His
perfection ! Our years ought to be bound each to
each by natural piety. The child should surely be
the father of the man.

> With age Thou growest more divine,
>   More glorious than before ;
> I fear Thee with a deeper fear
>   Because—I love Thee more.

I have been reading Moody's Life. It has much the
same effect as Finney's used to have in days gone by—
it creates a longing to work and live for God, to bring
men nearer to Him, to come nearer to Him myself.
Whom have I in heaven but Thee ? and there is
none upon earth that I desire in comparison of Thee.

What a wonderful thing that we, as a family, are
so united—that our Ideal is so much the same—
isn't it ?

To F. S. H.

St. Moritz: January 6, 1901.

I have succeeded in unfreezing my ink, so I can write and—although it is late to do so—wish you a happy new century. It is only once in a lifetime that one can do that sort of thing! I am out here for my health. I wasn't up to much last term. However, I am as fit as a lord now, and return to Cambridge this week. I have been reading out here two very different kinds of books. One is Wellhausen's 'History of Israel,' the other Moody's Life by his son. Wellhausen's book gives you in outline the position of modern advanced criticism of the Old Testament. I have never before studied the history from the critical point of view really seriously. The study has proved extraordinarily interesting, and I must say that in the main I agree thoroughly with Wellhausen's position. You will see it more or less clearly put in that 'History of the Hebrew People' in two small volumes by Kent which I recommended to you before. The history of the gradual progress of the divine revelation to the human race is a marvellous study : the way in which that people were educated to become the teachers of the world is utterly different from anything which we should have devised. I am struck more and more by the marvellous fact that God can and does reveal Himself—in His essential moral nature—to man ; that we are so made that we can apprehend the revelation ; nay, that we in turn can in measure reveal Him to men !

Moody's Life stirs me up to realise more the worth

of the individual, the surpassing value of man's moral and spiritual nature. I long to help men to see what I see, to love Him whom I love, and the failure of my efforts is largely, I feel, due to defects in myself. Still I do not despair of doing something.

To his brother Edward in South Africa.

Brislington, Bristol : April 10, 1901.

I was much interested in . . . (your letter) and in seeing a little into your life. There is a strange family reserve among us which I sometimes deplore. Perhaps it must always be so, that we can tell most readily to strangers our deepest thoughts and feelings. Yet I feel that we ought, as far as we can in this short life, to understand one another. We have been led by different paths to understand different aspects of Truth. Yet, when we have climbed to the top of the hill, I dare say we shall find that our paths were nearer to one another than we ever realised. At any rate, we shall meet on the top. I often think that your whole method of gaining truth must be unlike mine. I use my reason, but I am more than half affection, and it is that which helps me most. My strange love for some men makes me seek to live their lives, to see the world as they see it; above all, it forces me to pray. Prayer never seems to me irrational ; yet I do not pray so much because my reason bids me as because my affection forces me. I sometimes feel that I should go mad if I didn't or couldn't. And then, again, I am incapable of telling them all I feel, and I have to find some one to tell it to, and I feel forced back on One who knows me through and through, and I find comfort in pouring out my soul to Him—in telling Him all, much that I dare say to no one else—in letting Him sift the good and evil—in asking Him to develop and satisfy the good, and to exterminate the evil. I cannot help trusting Him.

> I know not where His islands lift
> Their fronded palms in air ;
> I only know I cannot drift
> Beyond His love and care.

You will tell me perhaps that I am too much like a woman in matters of faith. Yet so I am made. I must follow the lead of my whole being—not of my mind alone. I often wonder how it is that I love with such a strange, passionate, unutterable affection, and whether many men are like me.

I am most pleased to hear of your doings, especially of your whist parties.

To F. S. H., chaplain on board H.M.S. Canopus.

Brislington : April 10, 1901.

I am glad that you like your ' parish.' I feel more and more that I should prefer being among sailors to being among soldiers. I am afraid that I should do little good among either. Still I like, or think that I should like, naval officers even more than army officers. If they do talk a great deal of 'shop,' that is a healthy sign. I only wish our officers in the army were—I will not say more proud of their profession (for they have, I dare say, suffi-

cient pride)—but more anxious to learn and to think
out matters connected with it. I dare say the naval
officer is obliged to act more independently and to
think for himself in an emergency; for the army
discipline is carried to such an extreme that the man
for some years has seldom any occasion to act on
his own initiative—to rise to an occasion. He simply
has to ask a superior what to do next. He tends to
resemble the Hindu station-master who telegraphed
'Tiger on platform; please wire instructions.' If their
talking shop is worrying occasionally, yet be of good
comfort, it is on the whole a good sign. It is better
than talking golf or polo all day, and better far than
loose and unmanly conversation. The more you are
interested in the matters yourself, not simply because
you want to be all things to all men, if by any means
you may gain one or two, but because you are a man
and a Christian, and therefore all things human have
an interest to you, the more you will enjoy such
'shop.' We want not only to affect an interest in
what is of vital concern to our neighbours, but to
feel it. I begin to realise more now than I used to
that I must not simply watch football matches, or
run with the boats, because I want to show interest,
but because I am learning—however late in the day
and however imperfectly—to feel a real concern for
such matters. And, strange to say, I am more
interested in them than I used to be. Since the
Lord took human flesh and interested Himself in all
human life, He has left us an example that we may
follow in His steps. We must call nothing, and no
man, common or unclean. My own life and my own

interests are terribly contracted. Sometimes I have been foolish enough to glory in the fact, and to think that I honour God in caring only for my brother's soul and not for his whole life. But love has taught me that this is a low and incomplete view. God numbers the very hairs of our head, and he who loves and tries to help another must enter into his life and care for all that he cares for. I hope that God will spare me a little longer to work in College, and to learn to become one with others—to see life with their eyes, to let them teach me—that so, if it please Him, I may gain some of them for His service.

The disciple cannot expect to be above the Master. The Master was not popular. He explained His deepest teaching to a few—a very few. If you have one or two to whom you can explain part of your being, thank God. You will find that one man understands one side, another appreciates another side. It is a comfort that there is One who knows us through and through. What a terrible blank life would be if we had no God to whom to pour out our whole soul! There are sides of our being which no one but God seems to be able to apprehend. I am feeling now comfort at nights in simply telling Him all—feelings which I cannot explain to any one else, asking Him to interpret, to sift, to allow the better to live, to annihilate the untrue. I do not cease to expect great things from Him, to expect that He will do for my 'parish' as a whole more than I have dreamed of or wished for. But then I am content if He works slowly, and does what I did not wish or expect to happen. He works slowly in nature, and I am not surprised if human nature is still more stubborn material for Him to work upon. But what a joy it is when one character in which we are interested, for which we have prayed and wrestled in prayer, shows slight but sure signs of healthy development! I feel inclined to shout for joy at the miracle—for it is a miracle—and I thank God and take courage. He does not let us see many results, but He lets us see just enough to help us to go forward. It is a help when what is clear and true to us begins to dawn upon another. ' My belief gains infinitely,' says Novalis, ' when it is shared by any human soul.'

Let your ' parish ' clearly see that ' it is one thing to be tempted, another thing to fall.' Vile, foul thoughts which come to us are not in themselves a sign that we are falling. They are first of all from outside, and are suggestions entirely alien in origin from ourselves ; they are from the devil. They only become wrong when entertained, when welcomed in the least degree as guests and allowed to stay. Our aim is to bring every thought at once into captivity.

I have just come back from the seaside, and as I looked at the sea I thought more than once of ' the ocean of Thy love.' The waves of the sea beat against a stubborn rock and seem to make no impression. But in a few years' time the rock begins to yield. The constant wash of the waves wears it away So with our hard, stubborn wills. The ocean of His love will reduce them slowly but surely, and likewise the stubborn wills of men around us, thank God ! When you are tired and human strength gives way, remember 'the best of all is—God is with us.' I often feel worn out, and then I love, as it were, to lean back upon Him—without speaking—as a child on its mother's arms.

> I know not where His islands lift
>   Their fronded palms in air ;
> I only know I cannot drift
>   Beyond His love and care.
>
> O brother ! if my faith is vain,
>   If hopes like these betray,
> Pray for me that I too may gain
>   The sure and safer way.
>
> And Thou, O God, by whom are seen
>   Thy creatures as they be,
> Forgive me if too close I lean
>   My human heart on Thee.[1]

I am, I fear, but a poor friend. I wish you had some one who loved you as well as I did, and who was less weak and selfish. You must not give me up in spite of my defects. I love you and am proud of you—proud to think that you are doing work among men whom I should be powerless to influence. Easter once more brings new life and hope. May the God of all life, of all peace, of all hope, be with you and all your flock ! May He guide pastor and sheep ! Don't despair ; go on manfully ; you are doing greater work than you know, and if your eyes were open that you could see, you would find that the host that was with you was more than all that were against you. Into His keeping I commit you. Good-bye. Your friend

FORBES.

[1] Whittier.

L

To W. O.

I am glad that the lot has fallen to you in fair places. 'It has been said with true wisdom that God means man not only to work but to be happy in his work. . . . Without some sunshine we can never ripen into what we are meant to be.' So writes Dr. Hort. I am reading his Life with great joy. He drank deep of life, and I want to do so also. I want to live in the present—in the sunshine of eternity. I feel more and more inclined to thank God for life and all the good things it brings, and for the friends He has given me, and the measure of strength and health to use in the service of man.

I had no idea where that Essay had gone. I suppose it is most immature and unsatisfactory ; yet the central idea, however imperfectly expressed, must surely be true. He took Manhood—in its weakness and strength—up into God. He was tempted. That thought helps me immensely. ' It is one thing to be tempted, another thing to fall.' We often accuse ourselves wrongly when foul thoughts spring up within us. They are temptations from without—from the devil. They only become sins when entertained as welcome guests. I have lately thought that Christ's life, like ours, was a life of faith, that it needed a real and constant effort of faith for Him to realise His relationship with the unseen Father. Here and hereafter human life is based on faith. If we get this idea into our minds, Christ's temptations become more real. They are temptations to faithlessness. I like your idea that Christ has entered into our manhood, into the phases (if there be such) ' of the life to come.'

Rest in the Lord. This thought comes home to me more than it used to do. I like to bring all the perplexities of life—the thoughts and feelings which I can explain to no one—of some of which I cannot say whether they are right or wrong, or where the right shades into wrong—and to leave them with Him to develop (if right), to sift, to correct. What a blank life would be without God! . . .

Easter brings fresh hope and life. It is glorious to begin existence in a world which has been redeemed. I am sure—since He rose and defeated death—we ought to trust to life, to delight in it. ' I am the Life.'

Breathe in the fresh air. It is one of the best gifts that the good God has bestowed upon us. We want fresh air not only in our lungs but all through, if I may say so, our being. I long to be more natural and happy—not that I wish for ' religious happiness,' but something quite different—the happiness which comes in the right exercise of power and in conscious dependence upon Him in whom we live.

In reply to a letter from H. P., a master at Clifton College, who was in doubt whether he ought to resign his mastership and go down to the College Mission in Bristol.

Christ's College, Cambridge : May 1, 1901.

I have not had time to think over the matter yet, but my first feeling is that you ought to be very slow to move. If men in your position, who feel keenly interested in the highest welfare of their pupils and long to influence them in spiritual matters, all go away to parish work, what is to become of our public school boys? Masters are only too anxious to leave for more 'directly spiritual' work, as they say. But in doing so they leave a work of exceptional difficulty and importance behind, and who is to take their place? I understand and appreciate your feelings, but I am not at all sure that you have any call to go.

How much directly 'spiritual' work have you with the boys? Could you, if you desired, get more?

I will pray over the matter. Do be slow before you decide to leave. I believe you ought to stay, although it may be more difficult to maintain your own spiritual life and ideals in a school than in a parish. You may be doing more good than you know. It is easier to find men to do parish work than to do school work of the highest kind.

There is a sermon of Lightfoot's in which he urges clergymen at the University not to go away, because it is hard to maintain their spiritual ideals at Cambridge, and because they seem to have so little direct spiritual influence. May not this apply to your work also?

To one about to be ordained.

Cambridge: May 1901.

It seems so clear to us that you have a call, that I find it hard to realise that you yourself are uncertain. But the very fact that you have been 'counting the cost,' and that you have no ecstatic joy at the prospect before you, encourages me. I am glad you realise the difficulties beforehand. What you don't fully see is the strength upon which you will be able to draw. I often think of those lines of Tennyson :—

> O living Will that shalt endure
> When all that seems shall suffer shock,
> Rise in the spiritual rock,
> Flow through our deeds and make them pure.[1]

That Will can transform our will, and the very weakness of our natural will is then a help. The strength is seen and felt to come from an invisible source : ' Thy will, not my will.'

The terrible need of men to fight against the forces of evil impresses me. The call is so loud on every side. And if men like you cannot hear it, I am driven almost to despair. . . . I often think of my father's words on his deathbed : ' If I had a thousand lives I would give them all—all to the ministry.'

The thought that gave me comfort at my own ordination was a text suggested to me by my brother : ' He had in His right hand seven stars.' In His right hand—we are safe there. I felt such a worm as I had never felt before. ' But fear not, thou worm Jacob.' . . . Don't look for happiness or peace at this time, but for the presence and power (whether felt or unfelt) of that God whom we both love and

[1] *In Memoriam*, cxxi.

try to love better. Do not persuade yourself that
you do not love God. You do, more than you have
any idea of. The part of your 'Ego' which you
would least wish to lose is not even your love for
men—but for God. If you had your choice now,
and had to decide what part of your being you would
retain for eternity, it would be the latter. Beloved,
if our heart condemn us, God is greater than our
heart. . . . 'He who loves makes his own the
grandeur that he loves.'

He had in His right hand seven stars. He is
the Judge, but He also is our refuge and strength and
hope.

To D. B. K.

Cambridge : July 1901.

When we set to work to help others we discover
something of our own weakness. But along with
that discovery comes the realisation of an inexhaustible fund of strength outside ourselves. We are
fighting on the winning side. God must be stronger
than all that opposes. It is uphill work, especially
at first. But just as in learning a language or learning how to swim, after toiling on with no apparent
result, there comes a day when suddenly we realise
that we can do it—how we know not : so it is in
spiritual matters. There is effort still, sometimes
gruesome effort ; but it is all different from what it was.
We find the meaning of the paradox, 'Whose service
is perfect freedom.' Love takes the place of law,
and, although it is hard at times to serve God, it is
still harder to be the permanent servant of Satan.

Your enthusiasm ought to increase, the more you look life in the face and see its sin and misery. ' God,' said Moody, ' can do nothing with a man who has ceased to hope.' Our hope in the possibilities of the individual and of society ought to grow brighter and saner as time goes on. . . . Missionary work—I have often wished to do it myself, but have been ' let hitherto.' . . . It is a tremendous help to me to know that we are both serving the same Master and that I can trust you to His love.

To an Auckland ' brother' after Bishop Westcott's Death.

Cambridge : August 1901.

My thoughts are with you at this time. I am most thankful that you have been a year with that man of God, and have gained ideals and inspiration for work which will haunt you all your life long. In moments of weakness, at times ' when your light is low,' the memory of his strenuous, holy life will be a power making for self-discipline and righteousness. And it is more than a memory. For he taught us by word and deed that we are all one man, that those who have realised what it is to belong to the body here will enter more fully into its life there. ' We feebly struggle, they in glory shine '—yet we are verily and indeed one. That thought is often a comfort to me. When I feel the contradictions and perplexities and weaknesses of my own life, I love to think that I am part of a whole—that I belong to

the same body and share in the same spirit as some
other man who is immeasurably my superior.

When one whom we have known and venerated
on earth passes to the eternal home, it seems more
like home than it was before. It is peopled not only
with countless saints of whom I have heard, but with
one whom I have known and seen, and hope to see
again. His prayers for us, his influence upon us
there are more effective than they could have been
here.

The great triumph of Christianity is to produce a
few saints. They raise our ideal of humanity. They
make us restless and discontented with our own lives,
as long as they are lived on a lower plane. They
speak to us in language more eloquent than words:
'Come up higher.'

To F. J. C.

Belvedere Hotel, St. Moritz: Sunday, December 15, 1901.

I feel more and more thankful that I have not
had to wait till the next world to know God's true
nature and character and will. It is passing strange
that He should love us so much, and wish to unveil
Himself to us, 'that we might be a kind of firstfruits
of His creatures.' But that phrase 'stewards of
His mysteries' almost appals me. A steward must
be faithful, and must render an account of the way
in which he has used his master's goods. God grant
that at the final reckoning we may not be found un-
profitable servants.

How those simple words in the twenty-third
Psalm satisfy us more and more as life advances,

and as we realise that He is not our Shepherd only, but the chief Shepherd of the whole flock, and that He has yet other sheep whom He is looking for, and whom He will teach to hear His voice amid the babel tongues of the world. It is a comfort to me to feel that He has no private blessings for me apart from the rest of the family—that we are one in Him, and that each blessing unites us not only to the Head of the family, but to all the brothers within it.

I suppose at first it is hard to realise the unseen world for long together. But gradually that world dominates our being, and interprets the world we see, and makes all life intelligible and well worth the living.

To H. J. B.

Hotel Belvedere, St. Moritz : December 16, 1901.

I feel a new man now in this fresh mountain air. If I always lived here I might be good for something. What a parable of life! If we could live in the higher world and breathe in its air, what strong, healthy men we should be! I stayed a night once with Westcott, and it seemed to me that he lived and moved and had his being in a higher region, to which I now and then came as a stranger, and he could see habitually, what I sometimes saw, the way of God in human life. I am sure we are meant to have our home in that higher world, and that we only see life sanely, steadily, and in its true proportions, when we view it from that vantage ground. I have always been thankful that I spent that night with Westcott, and thereby gained, not simply fresh inspiration, but a radically new revelation of human life and its possibilities. It gave me an insight into the dignity and the destiny of our common human nature.

You have never been long absent from my thoughts, and at last I have had time and strength to begin to pray for you as I could wish. It is the only way in which I can show my gratitude to you. I don't understand much about prayer, but I think of that strange, bold parable of the unrighteous judge and the widow, and I take my stand on that. I shall not be content until your true self is formed ; and I think that God must be very ready to answer the prayer, however imperfect its form may be, of one who loves another more than he can understand. I like St Paul's words : τεκνία μου οὓς ὠδίνω μέχρις οὗ μορφωθῇ Χριστὸς ἐν ὑμῖν. Only I wish I were not such a worm myself. However, the thought of you compels me to live a better life. If I could only make all my thoughts of you into prayers and actions for you I should be more content.

Don't imitate Uriah Heep with ' Yours most humbly.' I won't stand that nonsense ! and you give yourself away just a few lines above, when you assert that you are too proud to confer a favour on me, and read Greek Testament with me. What a funny chap you are ! Can't you see, you idiot, what a pleasure you give me ? We shall have to compromise, and I'll have to make some concession to your pride. Neither —— nor I know much about your section, but we could help you in your first part papers. Of course, he could do it miles better than I can ; but, all the same, you are going to be my pupil. Promise me that you won't make any arrangement with him until you have talked the matter over with me. I'll make some compromise for the sake of your miserable pride, you wretched creature.

Write to me soon again, if it isn't a great bore. I can't recall as much as I could wish of your conversations with me. In fact, I have the unpleasant feeling sometimes that I did too much of the talking ! But one or two things that you said to me live in my memory, and make me wish to be more fit to talk to you.

St. Moritz is much as usual. It is a strange little world in itself. The comic and the tragic are blended weirdly together, and nature is unimaginably beautiful. I wish you could see this snow. It has an attraction for me, and I am sure it would have for you. I think you understand more about the meaning of beauty than I do. When I see a magnificent landscape, I want to share the sight with some one else. I feel quite lonely when I am interpreting it alone. I wonder why that is ?

To F. J. C.

Hotel Belvedere, St. Moritz : December 21, 1901.

Christmas seems to mean more to me, the longer that I live. I gaze with bewilderment on that stupendous mystery of love—the very God entering into and raising our human nature. My whole conception of the meaning, the possibilities of our common human nature is transformed, as I see that it can become a perfect reflection and manifestation of the Divine nature. 'The Word became flesh, and lodged *in us*.' The manger at Bethlehem reverses all our human conceptions of dignity and greatness. 'The folly of God is wiser than men.' It is to the humble—to babes—that God can reveal Himself. In them He can find His home.

> O Father, touch the East and light
> The light that shone when Hope was born.

It is in Christmas that Tennyson found the birth of Hope. It is Christmas that, as life goes on, bids us never despair—of our own or of human nature around us.

To a friend at Cambridge.

Hotel Belvedere, St. Moritz: December 30, 1901.

I shall never forget this last Christmas Day, for your letter came in the evening. I read it again and again, and wonder at it more each time I read it. I can't tell you what I feel about it. I knew that you more or less liked and respected me, but I didn't know that you loved me. I've got what I wanted. When you merely respected me, I dreaded the day when you would find that I was different to what you thought I was. But now I feel I am safe φόβος οὐκ ἔστιν ἐν τῇ ἀγάπῃ, however imperfect you find me. I know now that I can trust you not to throw me off. And love is not extreme to mark what is amiss, ὅτι ἀγάπη καλύπτει πλῆθος ἁμαρτιῶν. I can't thank you for your kindness, but I thank God for giving me the most precious gift in the world, a human soul 'to love and be loved by for ever.' As I look at your letter I feel a mere worm, and my one wonder is how on earth a man like you can call me your friend. I can't thank you; but I'll do my best to live up to the standard you expect of me, and to be a true friend to you. And my idea of friendship is, as you know, prayer. I can't, worse luck, do much for you, but I do pray for you, and 'whatever ye ask in prayer, believing, ye shall receive.' It has been truly said that the *how*, the *where*, and the *when* are not told us, but only the *what*. And I am quite certain that every prayer I offer for you is heard and answered, when I believe what I say; but the manner, the place, and the occasion of the answer—of these things I know nothing. I am sure that God loves to see us happy, and the pure joy of the knowledge that such a man as you loves me is almost more than I can bear. It throws a new light on life here, and on that fuller life to which God is leading us hereafter; like you, thank God, I cannot complain of lack of friends, but I have never had one who has written me such a letter, full of an affection for which I crave. The worst is, I can't repay your kindness. You bring me nearer to God, you make me realise in the strangest way His affection, you make me feel the worth and mystery of a human soul. I wish I could return your help somehow or other. Do show me the way. I wish you did not find it so difficult to pray for me. I am sure you are right in going back to such a man as St. Paul for subjects of prayer. The opening chapters of his letters to the Ephesians and Colossians give the kinds of requests which it is worth making on behalf of any one. There is surely no harm in finding that, as you pray for another, your own faith is growing. There is nothing selfish in that. It is rather the result of the law δίδοτε καὶ δοθήσεται ὑμῖν.

Your faith can only grow with exercise, and you exercise it by praying for others. You would only be selfish if you prayed for some one else *in order that* your own soul might be benefited.

But don't think too much of selfishness. Bring all your half selfish desires to Him who knows us through and through ; and in His presence, almost unconsciously, your motives will gradually be purified. You will learn to walk in the light as He Himself is in the light. As I look back on this letter, a large part of it seems selfish. I expect much is ; but, even in the selfish parts, there is something more besides. I can only just say what I feel, and ask God gradually to eliminate what is wrong. In His light I shall see light.

Life is large, and I am fearful lest, in attempting a rough and ready asceticism, I should exclude as wrong some elements which are in reality God-given. I feel that in the case of our affections and our longing for beauty. They are implanted in us, and tended and watered by One who is perfect Love and perfect Beauty. They easily lead us into sin, but that fact does not imply that they are wrong in themselves. We have to bring them to their source that He may interpret them. ' Too late have I sought thee,' said Augustine, ' thou Beauty, so ancient and so new, too late have I sought thee.' I cannot understand the mystery of your life, dearest, but I feel that all that craving for beauty is in some kind of way a craving for God. Only God demands the first place in your life before He will give you any satisfying interpretation of that aspect of His life. You must love Him for what He is—not simply because He is Beauty.

> I slept and dreamed that life was Beauty,
> I woke and found that life is Duty.

They are not really contradictory conceptions. Nay, Duty has a spiritual beauty of her own. But sometimes they seem for a moment divergent, and then you must at all costs choose the latter, and you will find that

> The topmost crags of Duty scaled,
> Are close upon that shining tableland
> To which our God Himself is shield and sun.

And, if I am not mistaken, that land will be utterly full of an absolutely satisfying beauty.

But I feel that I scarcely yet understand anything about the meaning of Beauty. All I can do is to relate it immediately to God. If I see beautiful scenery, I am usually thinking of God and thanking Him. If I see human beauty, I feel that I am on holy ground, and I always try to pray for a face that attracts me. I feel that I have a duty in return for the revelation that has been given. But, as you see, I can explain but little. These are merely rules of practical life which we very imperfectly carry out. I cannot explain the relation of physical and spiritual beauty in human beings. I feel, of course, that there ought to be, there very often is, some such relation. But sometimes there is something utterly wrong, and apparently no such connective. The connection, I take it, is more perfect in nature; but in man, why, something has occurred, something anomalous, which mars the whole. Sin has come in somewhere, I suppose.

I can't express on paper what I feel, or give you any real conception of what you are to me. You would be startled if you knew. God bless you, and work out in you, not my miserable ideal of what I think you ought to be, but His own ideal, which exceeds all our thoughts and imagination, of what you are to be.

To G. J. C.

Christ's College : 1901.

. . . I was never so pleased to hear of any engagement as of yours. I thank God with all my heart. I cannot put my joy into words, but somehow or other it seems to bring me nearer to the source of all joy. I feel more than ever that He cares for us and is educating us, and I feel that He has been so good to you, because He loves you. The older I grow the more I am impressed by His infinite sympathy and concern for us. And when He gives us not only love but a return of love, it seems to me that He is giving us the very best thing that He has —a part, as it were, of Himself. 'The merciful and gracious Lord hath so done His marvellous works, that they ought to be had in remembrance.'

I cannot tell you how glad I am. But I thank

God in my prayers for you; and I am sure that if
He has been so good to you in the past, He will not
forget you in the future.

*To the same when he had just accepted a mastership
at Eton.*

. . . . How good of you to write and tell me of
your future work ! . . . The responsibility of such a
life is to my mind almost overwhelming. 'Who is
sufficient for these things? Our sufficiency is of God.'

I am thankful that the offer came as it did—un-
sought by you. You will feel happier in accepting it.
'Infinite sympathy is needed for the infinite pathos
of human life '—more especially of a boy's life. The
first, second, third, requisite for a master is, in my
judgment, sympathy. As I look back on my own
school days, I cannot help feeling that most of my
masters were either lacking in it or else strangely incapable of manifesting it in a form which I could
understand. Sympathy with the dull, unpromising
boy is a divine gift, and I trust that Holy Orders
will confer upon you this grace also. I thank God
that you are taking orders, and finding your work in
teaching. Forgive this lecture from one who has no
right to speak, and who is himself strangely deficient
in sympathy.

To D. B. K.

I am glad that you have been home. I feel that
home is a revelation—a means whereby the Eternal
Father shows us Himself and His purposes, a

M

strengthening and refreshing of our tired souls. . . . I have prayed earnestly for you that your faith and love may not fail. I feel intensely the same difficulty as you, and I am only slowly learning to overcome it. I do not think we can learn to love people who are altogether different from us in many respects, all at once. I love some men with a strange, unsatisfied affection. All my thoughts about them I am gradually learning to resolve into prayers for them, and I want to live longer that I may pray for them more.

Well, it seems to me that God gives us this affection that we may learn to do to others as we would do to these. I cannot pretend to care for many with whom I come into contact as much as I do for the few. But I can pray for them, and the feeling will more or less come in time. Just try to pray for some one person committed to your charge—say for half an hour or an hour—and you will begin really to love him. As you lay his life before God, as you think of his needs and hopes, and failings and possibilities, as you pray earnestly for him as you would for some one whom you feel intense affection for ; at the end of the time you will feel more interested in him, you will think of him not as one of a class but as a separate, mysterious person. You will not, it may be, have time to pray for many in this way, but you will learn imperceptibly to extend your sympathy—to feel real love for many more. I advise you to keep a record of these prayers. It is quite worth your while to take practically a day off sometimes, and to force yourself to pray. It will be the best day's work you have ever done in your life. Remember that !

Don't be troubled by comparing yourself with other clergymen. I think you are like me—not ecclesiastically minded. I don't have the sort of feelings which a large number of persons have about their work and their preaching. I can't put the difference into words, yet I feel it. But I must serve God in my own way, and I am sure that He will use me to do the work for which I am best fitted. And the same is true of you. Try to refer all your actions to His standard; and test your work in His presence; and don't ask what So-and-so thinks of it.

I very much wish you had some gentlemen to associate with besides parsons. You must keep up as much as possible with your college friends; and use every opportunity which reasonably presents itself of seeing some 'society.' God knows what is best for you at present.

God nothing does or suffers to be done
But thou wouldest do thyself, couldest thou but see
The end of all events as well as He.

I am sure that He will not forget you. He knows what is best for your development. It may be that He takes you away from friends that you may learn to pray for them more and to see Him more clearly.

I think you will influence many men whom a more ordinary parson would not touch. . . . I am quite certain that if you have infinite hope—hope against hope—you will be a tremendous power in the place where God has put you.

Get as much exercise as you can, and always get a clear day off in the week, and don't give up any of your old interests. Don't always read 'religious '

literature. . . . When the long day is done and we
stand before the judgment seat, I believe that many
will rise up and call you blessed. Only pray for individuals—for a long time together. To influence
you must love ; to love, you must pray.

To one about to be ordained.

Eastbourne : September 1901.

I shall indeed remember you on Sunday next.
The words of the lesson come home to me to-day—
καὶ εἴρηκέν μοι Ἀρκεῖ σοι ἡ χάρις μου· ἡ γὰρ δύναμις
ἐν ἀσθενείᾳ τελεῖται.

We are poor creatures, but there is Grace—and
we can come into contact with it—and that is all we
need. We may have failed in the past, but Christ
offers a new childlike life and endless hope.

I am glad to think that you will be returning to
your difficult post at Cambridge. I am sure that
you will return to it with fresh humility and courage
—ἐν πληρώματι εὐλογίας Χριστοῦ.

To W. D. H.

St. Moritz : January 4, 1902.

I hope that you are now less overworked than
you were in October. You must at all costs *make*
quiet time. Give up work, if need be. Your influence finally depends upon your own first-hand
knowledge of the unseen world, and on your experience of prayer. Love and sympathy and tact
and insight are born of prayer. I am glad you have
a Junior Clergy S.P.G. Association. Try to take an
intelligent interest in it, and mind you read a paper
before long.

To his brother Edward in South Africa.

Hotel Belvedere, St. Moritz : January 7, 1902.

I am glad to think that we are now in many respects agreed about the general question of the war. I suppose in any great historical upheaval there are at the time a number of people who are attempting to make capital for themselves out of the misfortunes of others ; there are many who are working for their own hand ; and yet, when we look back on the crisis and judge it as a whole in the calm light of history, we see that a large and rational purpose has been worked out. At the time of the English Reformation—as some one was saying to me lately, pointing the parallel which I am working out—there must have been a number of honest and pure souls who held aloof from the whole of what appeared to be political jobbery and fortune-making at the expense of religious sentiment. Yet now most of us feel that the movement could not have had the effects that it had, unless down below all there was a strong upheaval of the national conscience. You will no doubt see many defects in this historical parallel ; but the thought is at any rate suggestive, and full of what we require in these latter days— hope. Of course I feel that injustice, dishonesty, cruelty, selfishness are in no way palliated because they take cover and occasion in a real movement of national feeling.

I feel for you much in your work for examinations. It must come very hard with ill health and

in a hot climate, with the freshness of youth to some
extent passed.   But

> O well for him whose will is strong,
> He suffers, but he shall not suffer long ;
> He suffers, but he cannot suffer wrong.

It needs more courage than you were required to
show on the field of battle.   But the reward is sure.
I feel strongly that this life is but the prelude to
a larger life, when each faculty will have its full
exercise.

> Ah yet, when all is thought and said,
> The heart still overrules the head ;
> Still what we hope we must believe,
> And what is given us receive ;
> Must still believe, for still we hope,
> That in a world of larger scope,
> What here is faithfully begun
> Will be completed, not undone.

These words come from Clough—the soul of honesty.

To H. J. B.

Derwent Hill, Ebchester, Durham : April 14, 1902.

It seems to me a truism to say that we ought to
look at life in the light of eternity.   Only then does
the true significance of the meanest action in life
appear.   Life is redeemed from triviality and vul-
garity.   So far from worldly possessions losing their
value, and ordinary occupations appearing insigni-
ficant, their importance is realised as never before.
If man does not live for ever, his character and
actions seem of comparative unimportance.   If he
does live for ever, it is rational for him to look at

each action in the light of that larger life which he inherits. If something like class distinctions are eternal, it is an inducement so to use your distinctive privileges here in a worthy manner, that hereafter you may use them for nobler ends.

I have expressed myself badly, but you will see what I want to say. My relations to you surely become not less, but more important, when I realise that I am only beginning to know and love you here. The eternal element in them—the knowledge that there is throughout an implicit reference to a Third and Unseen Person in all that I say to you or think of you—fills me with a sense of awe, and makes the relations more real because more spiritual.

To the mother of his godchild, Margaret Forbes.

July 6, 1902.

I cannot tell you what a pleasure it was to see my godchild. . . . I feel she has a strength of purpose and a desire to know the truth which will fit her for high service in God's kingdom on earth. I pray for her, and I shall do so in the future with fuller understanding and with great hope. What God hath begun He will assuredly bring to perfection. I hope that some day she will learn to pray for Uncle Forbes. I should value her prayers. It is good to feel that in the midst of your weary time of weakness God has given you such a child as a pledge of His affection for you, as an assurance that He believes in you. To give you a little child to train for Himself is a proof that He trusts you very much. I do not know that He could have given a greater proof of His confidence in you. And it is God's implicit trust in us that draws out our trust in turn. We trust and love Him, because He first trusted and loved us. I wonder more and more at the way in which He trusts us. To allow us to suffer without telling us the reason, when He knows that we shall be inclined to think harshly of Him—that is, perhaps, the greatest proof that He believes in us. He can try our faith and perfect it by long-continued trial, because He knows that we shall respond, that we shall prove 'worthy to suffer.'

To H. J. B.

Christ's College, Cambridge : August 26, 1902.

The worst of seeing you for some time is that I feel it all the more impossible to live without you. I realise now as never before that you are out and away before me, and better than I am ; and yet I feel that you are part and parcel of my life. You mustn't be too hard on me if I can't come up to your ideal.

Intellectually the Hebrew and Greek ideals may be irreconcilable. Yet 'life is larger than logic ;' and practically we may become heirs of both ideals. The man who loses the world, who gives up all without any desire for gain, is often given the whole back again transfigured, glorified by sacrifice. To get you must forget. If you love God absolutely with all your being, you inherit the life that is as well as that which is to come. If all is not given you, yet enough is given for the development of character. But there must, it seems to me, be an

absolute sacrifice—a surrender of your whole being—
whatever the result may be. There must be no
calculation.

> High Heaven rejects the lore
> Of nicely calculated less and more.

You must love the Lord your God with all your
heart and all your mind : you must trust Him to do
the best by you. You say the Hebrew ideal does
not appeal to you. But I know better ; for you half
like me, and I am a Hebrew of the Hebrews !
There must be a dash of recklessness about the man
who gains the other world. ' All or nothing ' is the
requirement of the kingdom of Heaven. To gain
yourself you must throw yourself away—' lose your
soul.' You must have faith. ' He who loves makes
his own the grandeur that he loves ' is a sentence of
Emerson which consoles me when I think of my love
for you.

To a friend at Cambridge.

40 Upperton Gardens, Eastbourne : September 8, 1902.

I have been thinking of you. I keep myself from
becoming morbid by making most of my thoughts
into prayers for you. The glory—wonder—strange-
ness of being loved by a man from another and a
better world fills me with gratitude to God. Sometimes it seems a dream, and I half dread that I shall
wake up and find that you have ceased to care for a
worthless creature. But φόβος οὐκ ἔστιν ἐν τῇ ἀγάπῃ,
ἀλλ' ἡ τελεία ἀγάπη ἔξω βάλλει τὸν φόβον. I need
not fear. I know that you will love me, whatever
happens.

I want you to be one of the best men that ever lived—to see God and to reveal Him to men. This is the burden of my prayers. My whole being goes out in passionate entreaty to God that He will give me what I ask. I am sure He will, for the request is after His own heart. I do not pray that you may 'succeed in life' or 'get on' in the world. I seldom even pray that you may love me better, or that I may see you oftener in this or any other world— much as I crave for this. But I ask, I implore, that Christ may be formed in you, that you may be made not in a likeness suggested by my imagination, but in the image of God—that you may realise, not mine, but His ideal, however much that ideal may bewilder me, however little I may fail to recognise it when it is created. I hate the thought that out of love for me you should accept my presentation—my feeble idea—of the Christ. I want God to reveal His Son in you independently of me—to give you a first-hand knowledge of Him whom I am only beginning to see. Sometimes more selfish thoughts will intrude, but this represents the main current of my prayers ; and if the ideal is to be won from heaven by importunity, by ceaseless begging, I think I shall get it for you. But it grieves me to think that I can do nothing else for you. To receive so many favours from you, and to be incapable of doing more in return —this is what saddens me. I feel an ungrateful brute. You have brought new joy, hope, power into my life, and I want to show my gratitude. You would be doing me a real kindness if you would tell me how I could show it.

Don't think by what I have said that I simply care—as an ' Evangelical ' would say—for your ' soul.' Every part of your being—everything you do or say —all that you are—has a strange fascination for me. Only I feel that the whole of it is a revelation of God ; and I want that revelation to be clearer, truer, simpler. I am sure God does not only care for our souls. It is every part of our complicated being —all sides of our manifold life—that attracts Him. He loves our home life, our affection for the dear old Mother Earth which He made, our interest in the men and women whom He formed in His own image. He longs that all those interests should be developed —that we should live genuine, sane human lives. But true development here or elsewhere—the law of exis-tence in heaven or on earth—is life through death. ' Verily, verily, I say unto you, Except a grain of wheat fall into the earth and die, it abideth by itself alone ; but if it die, it beareth much fruit.' You must give up all. As I think of you, those words keep ringing in my ears : ' If any one cometh to Me, and hateth not his own father and mother, yea, and his own self also, he cannot be My disciple.'

I cannot tell you what they mean. You must find them out for yourself.

If I were a true disciple of Christ, you could see what they mean by looking at me. But I am not. You must learn their meaning for yourself. Your mother's life will speak louder than words of mine. Only I know they are true. Christ will recreate the world, recreate the home, human beings, dear Mother Earth ; but He cannot do so until you have been willing to give up all—until He has caused you to be 'born again.' When the ruler asked how these things could be, Christ could only repeat His words. The man must work it out for himself.

But I am sure that he that willeth to do the will shall know whether the teaching be true. There are no doubt some mere intellectual obscurities in the ideal which I might make simpler if I were not such a duffer. But finally a paradox would be left—a paradox which can only be solved by living the ideal out, and finding it work. It is the pathos of our love, of God's love for us, that each man, however much he is loved, must work out the ideal for himself. No man can save his brother's soul.

I do not like to weaken the paradoxes of the Gospel. I think there is more in Christ's words concerning 'loving one's life' or 'self' than you suggest. You say it means 'self-denial.' Yes, that is true, but what a tremendous meaning 'deny one's self' has! To disown your identity, that is not much easier when you come to think of it than to lose your life. I know you will find out what it all means, and that human love, beauty, home, social service, will be more real than ever before, because you will see the eternal reality underneath. You will be a 'new creation.'

Now I must stop without satisfactorily answering your question, without entering into any casuistical questions concerning conformity such as you suggest. I should like you to think out that problem in casuistry more for yourself, before I attempt to answer it. Forgive me for talking so much about myself. When all is said and done, words fail me. I can only thank God that you exist, and that you let me love you.

To H. P., a Clifton College master who had given up school work in order to devote himself to the School Mission in Bristol.

40 Upperton Gardens, Eastbourne : September 30, 1902.

. . . I am glad that you feel you have done right in giving up your school work. I am sorry that you left Clifton, but you thought you *ought* to go, and that is an end of the matter. I can only hope that you are in some measure a connecting-link between the school and its mission. . . . Don't forget me in my very different work—and yet work for the same Master—at college. I have need of your prayers. It is so easy to blunder, and to drive a man further from the kingdom by lack of sympathy and love. I feel more than I used to my weakness, and my absolute need of prayer.

To his brother Edward in South Africa.

40 Upperton Gardens, Eastbourne : October 1, 1902.

The October term has an interest of its own, bringing, as it does, a batch of freshmen. I try more and more not simply to impose my ideals upon them, but to find out their ideals and to quicken them with all my power. But assuredly 'infinite sympathy is needed for the infinite pathos of human life ; ' and my sympathies are as yet imperfectly developed.

Still, as years go by, I think I can sympathise more with those who have been trained up in other

schools of thought and experience. I was reading in
a book lately that we are largely responsible for our
own experiences, that we have a duty to get them of
the right kind. The book was by an American lady
on social questions. I think there is truth in her
words.

To D. B. K., head of a Public School Mission.

Eastbourne : October 1902.

I delight to know men better, because I find so
much more in them than I had expected. They
differ from me, and I try to get out of the habit of
making them in my own image, and try to find the
image in which God is making them. I have been
praying for you. I want a spirit of sanity and sacrifice to possess you, that you may be able to see the
good works which God has prepared beforehand that
you should walk in them. . . .

I am struck by the sacrifice which Christ demands.
Unless the man hates father, mother, family, friends,
yea, and himself also, he 'cannot be' His disciple.
Christ gives them all back again—only 'with persecutions.' We find more in the world, when we are
' crucified to it,' than ever before ; but there is a
something added. We have a deeper joy in home
ties, in human love, in social life, in the changing
seasons, in the dear old earth. Only the joy has a
note of sorrow, a pathos, which Christ calls 'persecutions.' We see more in life, and yet we are in a
measure out of sympathy with our surroundings.
We have heard and we can never forget the sorrows
of those who are ' one man ' with us. There is more

in that word 'persecutions' than this, as no doubt you have found. But this, I think, is part of its signification, isn't it? . . .

I believe in your 'mission' even more than you do. It is men like you, who through great tribulations strive to enter the Kingdom, that God uses. The fact that you are two men, and that the true man —the Christ—is painfully yet surely being 'formed' in you, means that you will be able to appeal to others who are painfully conscious of their double consciousness and are often the slaves of the lower, inhuman self. Your wealth of affection will make you feel as St. Paul did—τεκνία μου, οὓς πάλιν ὠδίνω μέχρις οὗ μορφωθῇ Χριστὸς ἐν ὑμῖν.

These words sum up for me, better than any others, my deepest wish for my friends. I fall back with desperate energy upon prayer, as the one power by which my wish can be realised.

You seem to look ahead almost more than is necessary. I delight in the feeling that I am in eternity, that I can serve God now fully and effectively, that the next piece of the road will come in sight when I am ready to walk on it. 'I do not ask to see the distant scene.' I hate the unsettled feeling that I have not yet begun my main work.

Don't measure work by human standards of greatness. Your present occupation might well be the envy of angels—if they could envy.

But now I am lecturing. So it is time to shut up. . . .

I fear that the origin of evil is more of a mystery to me now than when I wrote that essay! But I still think that we are fighting a real being, one whom we can best describe as personal. His will, it seems to me, must be given to him by God. He has identified it with a hitherto unrealised potentiality for disobedience. In plain language, his will is free, and therefore capable of resisting God. I should like to have a talk with you some day about it. But, as you see, the problem is beyond me. . . .

It is a strength to me to feel that you are fighting the devil in yourself and others up in ——, and that I am ' one man ' with you.

To D. B. K.

St. Moritz : January 1903.

It is getting on for your birthday, isn't it ? Congratulations. I wish I knew the exact day. I think more and more that a birthday is a subject not—as poor Job thought—for anathemas, but for congratulations. To be a reasonable human being—with capacity for seeing something of God's purposes for the race—with power to forward them—with opportunities for love and sacrifice and prayer—oh ! I am so glad that I was not a mere animal. And to be born at the end of the nineteenth century—I prefer that period even to Apostolic times. We can know more of God's purposes, enter more deeply into His mind and even His heart, than primitive Christians.

I have been reading to-day Temple's essay on 'The Education of the World' in 'Essays and Reviews.' Get hold of an old copy of that book, and read it. It is strong and manly, and rings true. I love that old man with his tenderness, simplicity, thoughtfulness, and will of steel. I thank God for him. There is something about utter goodness which makes me worship, and fills me with the challenge, 'Go and do thou likewise.' Goodness is as infectious as any disease.

I have been thinking lately of the self-sacrifice of God's life. I suppose that is the reason why He can enter into our lives—see them from the inside.

> Thou canst conceive our highest and our lowest,
> Pulses of nobleness and aches of shame.

It must have been the wealth of His self-sacrifice which made Him give us selves—wills—of our own. Then He makes them His own by more self-sacrifice. We are made in His image—made to go out of self, and find our self by losing it. Other men at first seem to limit our freedom, but later we find that the apparent limitations are only just scope for realising our true self. Each time we go out of self, and enter into another 'ego,' we return the richer for our sacrifice. We take up other lives into our own, and are richer than a millionaire.

I think that when the other 'ego' is most unlike our own—when at first sight the man is repulsive, and (worse still) uninteresting to us—when the sacrifice is great, if we would see life through his eyes, share his ambitions, fears, longings, and mental outlook, then is the time when we are peculiarly rewarded for our pains. Our consciousness is larger, more human, more divine than before.

'By feeblest agents doth our God fulfil His

N

righteous will' is the thought suggested by some of our brother-clergy. God does not choose the agents we should choose. Or perhaps the latter do not respond to His choice. Yet I feel that I am one of them, and that it is my faults writ large which I detest in them. I feel that, with all the riches of the revelation which I possess, I have that same self-satisfaction and lack of sympathy which I loathe in others. It is my life which is the stumbling-block to my message. They have often far less light than I have, but walk in it more simply than I do. The rafter in my own eye troubles me even more than the speck in theirs. But it is hard, God knows, sometimes to feel His presence in their presence. But the forces of good must be united (' Keep, ah ! keep them combined. Else . . .'), and if by any effort we can enter into their lives, and transcend the barriers between us, we are not only enriching our own life, but we are doing our best to show a combined front against the almost overwhelming forces of evil.

Even the Apostles must have found it hard to work together. We know they did. Look at Peter and Paul. Yet the Spirit of unity was stronger than all that opposed Him, and the One Body was in some measure realised. What was difficult in the childhood of the Body is still more difficult in its manhood. And Englishmen, with their strong sense of individuality, find it a terrible lesson to learn.

But pray. You enter then into another man's ' ego.' You see him in God. You see him as an end in himself. Remember Kant's maxim—a wonderful maxim from one who would not, I suppose, be technically called a Christian—'Treat humanity, whether in thyself or in another, always as an end, not simply as a means.' Put aside a certain amount of time, and pray for one man. If your thoughts wander, do not be disturbed, do not try to find when they began or how they began to wander; do not despair, go back to the subject in hand. And God will have mercy. Your influence, your life, your all, depends on prayer.

We must faint sometimes. But let your saddest times, your deepest struggles be known to God. Gain there the strength and quietness which you need for life. But don't let men see the agony—let them see the peace which comes from wrestling alone with God—wrestling for them.

You are not one man, but two or three. Thank God for that. It means that you will have a hard life—an awful struggle with self or selves: but it also means more influence, more power to enter into man's life. So many of the finest men owe their attractiveness to their diverse, many-sided nature. You will be able to feel for such, and perhaps to help them. You are half a Greek with your yearning for beauty and knowledge, half a Hebrew with your loathing for sin and love of God. The Greek in you must not be annihilated, but it must be subordinated to the Hebrew. Conscience must be absolute master. You must sacrifice the 'Greek' to Christ; but He will give you back what is best in the Greek ideal, all the better for the mark of the Cross on it. He will give it you back partly in this world, partly in the next, when you have learnt to renounce it—if need were, for ever—for His sake. But you must give up all for Him without thought of reward. He can give no reward to the man who is looking for it. The thought of your life helps me. Go on, for the night cometh when no man can work. Thank God it is yet day.

To his brother Edward in South Africa.

Mühlen, Switzerland : January 11, 1903.

I found walking a pleasant change after reading philosophy, which I have been doing during my holidays. I seem to have been getting my ideas a little clearer, and am no longer as content as I was with the Kantian doctrine, that our knowledge in speculative matters never gets beyond 'appearances.' I feel that at every turn we do get to that which *is*— to an underlying reality. I cannot feel that Kant's hard and fast division between 'speculative' and 'moral' reason holds good. The external world, because it is intelligible, must be akin to us; there must be an intelligence in it, otherwise it would never become an object of knowledge to our intelligence. It is not only in our ethical life that we come across the absolute consciousness. I feel now more than ever how we cannot divide up ourselves into water-tight compartments, and think of reason, will, and feeling as separate things, lying side by side. They can be separated—abstracted—in thought, but in actual life you never find one without the other. We cannot think without some degree of attention, and attention involves an exercise of will, and will cannot be exercised without desire, and desire involves feeling.

I think faith also cannot be regarded as a separate faculty. Reason, will, and feeling are all involved even in the faith of a poor cottager ; much more does reason enter into the faith of a thoughtful man.

I have been reading Butler, and hope when I go back to study Hume. What a wealth of light the conception of 'Development' has shed upon the problems which exercised the eighteenth century ! I have read half through Leslie Stephen's 'Thought in the Eighteenth Century,' and I have been struck again and again at the new aspect that the old questions take when looked at from the standpoint of Evolution.

I feel also that we need to study more the evolution of *thought*—the necessary phases that reason (like man's physical life) must pass through before perfection. . . .

I think you are right, that education must now include instruction in imperial ideas—in our relations with that larger social life which is dawning upon us —a step towards a still larger social life to be realised in the brotherhood of nations.

To F. J. C.

Christ's College, Cambridge : February 1, 1903.

I am slow to suggest to another man that what seems bad luck is in reality the voice of God making itself felt in his busy life, calling him to fuller sacrifice. But I am sure that we are right when we interpret it thus for ourselves. I share your wish for 'some really strong man' to come as a prophet and read the writing on the wall, and tell us 'what it all means.' Yet the absence of human help is not accidental. It must be designed, in order that we may learn to fall back on the everlasting arms—to find by experience that the unseen is more real than the seen.

> There is an arm that never tires
> When human strength gives way.

I like that phrase, 'worthy to suffer.' It is to those whom God loves best and most that He gives—as He gave to His Son—the chance of suffering. Sympathy, strength, reality—these are some of its fruits for those who allow them to grow. 'He cannot be My disciple.' I can't help sometimes thinking of these words. Unless the man is prepared to make sacrifice the basis of his life, he *cannot* be Christ's disciple. I don't think we always realise the 'transvaluation of values' found in Christ's teaching. 'Blessed are the poor—the hungry. He that would save his life shall lose it. He that loseth, saveth. He that would be greatest shall be least. It is more blessed to give than to receive.' As I think over such statements as these, I find that I have again and again to revise, as it were, my moral arithmetic —to change my standards, to revise my ideas of great and little, happiness and misery, importance and insignificance.

I am sure that nothing but the highest will satisfy you. God has given you singular powers of influence and of attracting others. He will demand an account of those powers. You know Matthew Arnold's lines on his father. I believe the day will come when men will say like words of you.

> But thou would'st not *alone*
> Be saved, my father ! alone
> Conquer and come to thy goal,
> Leaving the rest in the wild. . . .
> Therefore to thee it was given
> Many to save with thyself.

That is what I want you to be—a tower of strength —strength perfected, it may be, in weakness—weakness forcing you to despair of self, and find the Rock of Ages. You have been so much to me, and helped me so often, that I feel you must be born to help others as well. And this quiet time, it may be that God is using it to call you closer to Himself, to teach you to revise your 'values,' to show you a new fund of strength.

> Our wills are ours, we know not how,
> Our wills are ours, to make them Thine.

You must—literally must—let His will overpower your will. Nothing but complete sacrifice will satisfy you or Him, and I believe in you profoundly. I am sure that, whatever be the ghastly struggle, you will go through with it, and find your strength in Him. I pray for you.

To his mother.

Cambridge : March 15, 1903.

The term is almost over . . . I am enjoying a quiet Sunday. What a blessing these Sundays are to us—a foretaste of a fuller life of service and worship hereafter! I have been thinking lately with comfort of the quiet perpetual work of the Holy Spirit, silently but surely leading us on to higher things—comforting, correcting, guiding. It gives ground for hope in dealing with men, this knowledge that there is One who perfects what we feebly struggle to begin, who watches over men with a love that will not let them go. We are not alone in our work; we have omnipotence and illimitable wisdom on our side, forwarding our efforts. When I consider what the Spirit has accomplished in my own life, I have large hope for others. The argument from personal experience is singularly convincing. 'The fellowship of the Holy Ghost'—it is He who unites men and interprets them one to the other. It is He who gives spirit and life to our words.

To H. J. B.

Bexley House, Cromer: March 31, 1903.

It was good of you to send me that card from Florence. You don't know how glad it made me. To know that you were thinking of me was a strength to me. Your love for me comes as a perpetual surprise and inspiration. I feel a brute compared with you, but the knowledge that you care for me more than you do for most men makes me feel that I must try to be good. 'In Italy of the fifteenth century renaissance we see in strange confusion all that we love in art, and all that we loathe in man!' Greek history was short compared with the Hebrew: I suppose because intellectual and artistic ideals are more easily realised than ethical and religious. It takes time to make a saint. It is part of the discipline of life to find the two sets of ideas apparently antagonistic. There is a higher unity in which they are blended—in God Himself. It must be right to follow the dictates of conscience when it bids us lose our soul if we would gain it. We cannot trust God too much. If we forget our self, He will see that our truest self is ultimately realised.

I can't express myself well, for I have just finished a spell of hard work. I have sent away my tripos papers to-night. I am going up to Edinburgh on Friday or Saturday. I fear I shall not see you until April 21. Will you tell Armitage that I will, if convenient to him, sleep at Westminster that night instead of going straight to Cambridge? The hopelessness of ever showing my gratitude to you or of ever making you realise how much I love you oppresses me. I don't know what I should do if I had not One Higher than I am to confide in—if I could not leave you in His hands—if I could not gain strength and life for you by appealing to Him.

O brother, if my faith is vain,
    If hopes like these betray,
Pray for me, that I too may gain
    The sure and safer way.

And Thou, O God, by whom are seen
    Thy creatures as they be,
Forgive me if too close I lean
    My human heart on Thee!

I lean closer and closer as life goes on. I feel that our hope lies in despair—despair of self. The vessels which contain the treasure are, as to-night's lesson says, earthen, ' that the excess of the power may be God's and not from us.' And there *is* a power, there is a life working in us. It is the quiet, sane, constant work of the Spirit in and upon our spirit, that never hastes and never tires : which gives me comfort for you, for myself, for all of us. The same life that is at work in the hedge across the road is in us, only in us it attains full self-conscious-ness and freedom. We can deliberately use it or refuse it. Forgive the length of the letter. But I felt so tired that I thought it would do me good to write to you, selfish brute that I am.

I expect you enjoyed your time in Italy im-mensely. I should have liked to be with you. I wonder if ever we shall be there together ? Some day we shall be in a world where the barriers of space are broken down : ' There shall be no more sea.' Yet it seems to me that we have not altogether to wait for that other world. They are half broken down already ; and if we had faith as a grain of mustard seed, we should realise tne meaning of a unity deeper than any special or temporal bond. If we fail to realise its meaning now, shall we realise it then ? Is not life here a training for life hereafter ? If we learn nothing in this school, we shall not be able to take our places in that school of ' broader love.' The best part in me does not complain. I thank God for His thought-ful goodness in bringing you near to me. I thank Him for the mystery of life, which enables me to realise that

Power 'which lives not in the light alone, But in the darkness and the light.' I become more and more inclined to thank Him as I see Him more clearly.

To F. S. H. on his accepting the post of chaplain at the Royal Naval College, Osborne.

Cambridge : April 30, 1903.

I am satisfied with your decision. I thought over the matter, but I could not see my way quite clearly to say anything more definite, so I did not write again. Don't think that my silence was due to slackness. I did what I thought was better than writing. I spent an hour in praying over the matter. Now that the matter is settled I can tell you what a keen pleasure it is to me to have my dear old —— near me in England,[1] and doing a piece of work which is full of hope and joy. I would not say this before, because I did not wish to influence your decision by private considerations. Get some quiet time for prayer before September 1, that when you go to Osborne you may go ἐν πληρώματι εὐλογίας Χριστοῦ ('filled full with the blessing of Christ'). I feel increasingly the need of such times to learn to walk by faith without stumbling, and to accustom myself to the atmosphere of faith, to see things as they appear to a man who has faith 'as a grain of mustard seed.'

Westcott records a visit (see 'Life,' i. 249) to his old schoolmaster, Bishop Prince Lee. '"People quote various words of the Lord," said the Bishop, "as containing the sum of the Gospel—the Lord's Prayer,

---

[1] He had been offered work in South Africa.

the Sermon on the Mount, and the like ; to me the essence of the Gospel is in simpler and shorter terms : μὴ φοβοῦ, μόνον πίστευε.[1] Ah! Westcott, mark that μόνον," and his eyes were filled with tears as he spoke.' Ah! S——, mark that μόνον! . . . God bless you in your new work and make you a blessing to others as you have been to me.

To A. E. K.

St. Thomas's Home, St. Thomas's Hospital :
August 28, 1903.

. . . I am most grateful for your kind words, though I know full well how little it is that I have done for you. We clergymen so often seem to be working in the dark. There are no clear results to show, as *e.g.* a doctor can comfort himself with, when he has visibly cured a patient. And I for one am too easily inclined to despair, and to wonder whether the work is not in vain. But 'trust is truer than our fears.' Yet it does me good when I feel I have done anything, however tiny, for a man. After all, results are best left in God's hand. He gives us enough to help us the next step onward, but not enough to exalt us, and to make us think we can do anything without His assistance. Work 'in the Lord' cannot be in vain.

I am glad you have been reading Bishop Westcott's life. He was a man of God, and his life is an inspiration, and a prophecy of what our life may—nay, some day—will be. . . . I like that passage

---

[1] 'Be not afraid, only believe.'

when he goes to see his old schoolmaster, Bishop Prince Lee, who tells him with tears in his eyes that to his mind the whole Gospel message is summed up in the words ' μὴ φοβοῦ, μόνον πίστευε.'

To a friend who had been an international athlete.

St. Thomas's Home : September 5, 1903.

We had a fairly good 'Long' in spite of the miserable weather. Congratulate me. I won my first athletic distinction last 'Long'—a ten-shilling prize. I am thinking of chucking work and becoming a professional. It was a second prize in a tennis tournament. I had (I must own) the best player in College as my partner. I want to get a very conspicuous object as prize. What do you suggest ?

To C. T. W.

St. Thomas's Hospital : September 1903.

I am getting on first-rate, and I hope to be up early next week. I believe you are right. We should do well if we had more regularity and self-discipline in our life at Cambridge, and we should have more power over others. Pray for me. . . .

You needn't pity me. I am having a very good time. It is jolly to do nothing, and not even to have to dress and undress—both exhausting and monotonous occupations. It has been a glorious day, and although it is almost 7 P.M., I am still out on the balcony enjoying the cool breezes.

To W. O.

Alassio : December 1903.

Death has come near to my family lately. I told you that my sister—the Deaconess—had passed away from us.[1] It is not all sorrow, when we know that the life has been spent in walking with God, when we know that this corruptible puts on incorruption, and that what is sown in intense bodily weakness is raised in strength—eternal strength.

I am so glad that God has given to you His highest blessing. I long to meet your future wife. It makes me very happy to think of the happiness in store for you—to know that you are in the best of all schools. I thank God. Love will bring you both nearer to the source of Love. . . . This new blessing, as you say, is 'the gathering up of the best that God gives.' I can't express my thoughts as I would, but I am very, very glad. . . .

Illness teaches one many lessons. I trust I have learned some. I have been amazed at the goodness of my friends !

To W. P., an officer in the Army.

Hotel Salisbury, Alassio, Italy : December 21, 1903.

I don't think things happen by chance. Indeed I am sure they do not. I have never felt so humbled to the earth. One sees one's life as a whole, when one is helpless and can do nothing, and the whole looks very poor and mean. It is like the judgment-

[1] His sister, Deaconess Cecilia, 'passed away' at the Deanery, Westminster, on September 8.

day—only with this grand exception, that life is not yet over, that the night has not yet come in which 'no man can work,' that you have still a chance to make the future better, more honest, more noble than the past. Then, again, I learnt the utter and wonderful kindness of my friends. I felt so selfish and so surprised at the goodness they showed me. Again, I saw something of the mystery of pain. My own was so trivial compared with that which some others had to bear. Yet I had enough to startle me that such a fact should be permitted on earth at all. I don't suppose we can understand its meaning; but my consolation was that it is not necessarily a sign of God's displeasure—that the highest life was a life of suffering, that the Son of Man was a 'Man of Sorrows.' Everything seems to me to depend upon the way in which one takes the pain—if one voluntarily says, 'Thy kingdom come, Thy will be done,' then one is entering into the highest life, and the pain becomes a new method of serving and knowing God. But physical pain, if prolonged, is a terrible thing; and there is no time on a bed of sickness for praying or thinking much of God unless one is accustomed to do so in health. The needs of the poor body press in upon one. Death-bed repentances are realities, but I am inclined to think that they are very rare. It is terribly dangerous to defer being good until we are ill. Illness does not necessarily make us good.

I am afraid I was but a poor coward, and yet my faith did not utterly fail. God is the one hope for a man who is ill, and He is true to His word. He hides His face behind the clouds; but even when I couldn't see Him at all, I felt that He was there. Pray for me; at present I feel too weak to pray much for myself. I want—I do want—to be a better man, to help others nearer the kingdom. I want, when life is over, to have a better record to look back upon than I had in hospital.

To F. S. H.

Alassio, Italy: January 2, 1904.

Your letter came to me at a time when I was rather low. I had to have a second operation. However, after fifteen weeks of Nursing Homes I escaped, and, as soon as I could, made my way to St. Moritz. For once the place didn't seem to suit me very well. So, after little more than a week, I came down into Italy. I am so far recovered now that I quite hope to be able to go back to college at the beginning of this term.

Illness and pain have taught me some lessons—at least I hope so. I feel solemnised, startled, when I think of how life looked when I could do nothing for the time. Pray for me that I may be more real. I learnt, too, how futile it is to put off repentance till sickness. It is hard at such a time to think of aught save self and physical pain. And my own pain was so trivial compared with that of others. O God! it is a terrible thing. Some day shall we be able to understand, if not with the head, with the heart, part of its meaning? Meanwhile the individual can say, however feebly, 'Thy kingdom come, Thy will be done.'

To his brother, a doctor in South Africa.

Alassio, Italy : January 7, 1904.

At last I am beginning to get tired of doing nothing. I hope that eventually I shall be stronger than I have been for some years past. At any rate I hope a little first-hand experience of pain will make me more sympathetic. Pain seems to me now a greater mystery than ever before. But I comforted myself with the thought that in the highest Life ever seen on earth, there was a full measure of spiritual, mental, and physical pain. Also it was a comfort to feel that when one accepted, not simply with resignation but with faith, certain suffering, one was in sympathy with the will of the universe, 'working together with God' in some mysterious way. What a strange place a hospital is ! How wonderful the Gospels are, with their hope and comfort on every page——hope for the physical as well as the mental side of man's life ! I like more than ever now to read how Jesus went about healing all manner of diseases and all manner of sickness and bringing life and strength wherever He came, showing us that Heaven is on our side in our wrestle with all that deforms and degrades human nature.

I certainly don't regret my illness. Besides showing me the marvellous kindness of friends, it has, I hope, taught me much.

O

APPENDICES.

I.

THE following letter addressed to the Editor of this volume was received from the Rev. H. Bisseker, chaplain at the Leys School, Cambridge, too late for insertion in an earlier portion of the book :

'Your brother's friendship, as you must have heard so often during the past few months, was valued in Cambridge beyond that of most men, and I am probably only one of many who still look to that friendship as among the prominent facts of their time up here. Though personally I did not learn to know Mr. Robinson when I first came up, his brotherliness so deeply impressed me during the four years for which our friendship lasted, that I still find it difficult to believe that he is no longer to be found in the familiar rooms at Christ's, and has ceased to be a part of our Cambridge life. And yet, in another sense, he has *not* ceased to be a part of that life ; for one feels that during his residence up here he managed, if one may so express it, to put a bit of himself into more than one man, and that in this way he will continue to live among us long after he himself has been removed.

'I have often thought about him and his quiet, strong influence since we heard that we had lost him, and almost invariably the same three of his characteristics assume the uppermost place in my thought. Different sides of his nature would appeal to different men : I can best serve your purpose by mentioning those which made the deepest impression on my own mind.

'One of the chief causes of your brother's influence was unquestionably *his sense of the value of the individual*. He used to take men one by one and make a separate study of each. The consequence was that he *knew* his men. On any given visit the acquaintance did not, as it were, have to be begun over again. On the contrary, the acquaintance once formed, some common ground already existed ; for so great was your brother's power of sympathy that, where at the first no such common ground appeared to exist, he soon learnt to find a standing-place himself on that assumed by the man he was seeking to know. And not only did Mr. Robinson possess this power of valuing the individual, but he also was able to inspire the objects of his influence with the knowledge of his particular interest in them. Thus they soon dropped the idea of acquaintanceship, and began to think of him as friend, and there you have in a word the secret of his wide influence. He was interested in *men*, but what he loved was *a man*.

'Mr. Robinson was no less marked off from the majority of men by the stress which he laid upon the reality and power of prayer. We used from time to time to have long talks together on this subject, so that I can speak with some little knowledge of the place which he assigned it in his life. With characteristic modesty he not infrequently distrusted himself in his active contact with men. His very anxiety to help others towards the ideals by which his own life was dominated led him to see the risk of placing hindrances in their way by an injudicious intrusion into the secret places of their hearts. Drawn in different directions, therefore, by his passionate desire to win men for Christ and his cautious fear lest untimely words of his should hinder rather than help, he found refuge in giving himself up to earnest prayer on their behalf. And prayer to him meant more than a light repetition of words. He used often, I believe, to spend as long as half an hour at a time in seeking blessing for a single man. We cannot doubt that, in the strong influence which he himself exerted upon so many of those who knew him, such persistent prayer received at least a part of its own answer.

'The last element in your brother's individuality which always impressed me was his restrained, but genuine, mysticism. In the few accounts of his life that I have read I do not remember any allusion to this characteristic. That he possessed it, however, and this to no usual degree, seems to my mind quite patent ; in fact, it was this suggestion of mysticism that first attracted me to him. The mysticism one sees around one is often so unregulated and so ignorant that it was refreshing to find a mystic who was also an enlightened scholar and thinker. It confirmed the feeling, instinctive in one's heart, that, despite the abuse of caricature, a deep, intelligent apprehension of unseen realities is of the essence of the fulness of religion. Mr. Forbes Robinson appeared to possess an unusually certain cognisance of the unseen world. How well I remember the way in which, again and again, tea over and our pipes lighted, he would curl himself up in one of his or my own big chairs and discuss questions of interest to us both with a far-away look in his eyes altogether suggestive of a genuine otherworldliness! And this familiarity with unseen verities seemed to run through all those parts of his life with which I was acquainted, and indeed to be to him the most real fact of all existence. To use the simple language of olden days, I believe that " he walked with God ": and that explains his life.

'These, then, were the three characteristics of your brother which more than any others have impressed themselves upon my mind. I do not think that they were three separate sides of his personality: I should say, rather, that they were three different expressions of one fundamental attribute. It was because he walked so closely with God that he so loved the individual sons of God. It was because he so loved the Great Father and each child of His that he had so strong a faith in the power of prayer and such unwearying patience to persist in it.

'A life like your brother's, if I may say one thing more, forms, I sometimes think, one of the strongest pledges of human immortality. In one sense, it is true, he seems to have done so much; and yet, in another sense, those of us who knew the faculties which he had cultivated, his knowledge and patient

scholarship, his sympathy and insight, his tact and
passion for men, and, most precious of all, his power
with God, were looking for even greater things in
years to come. Such fitness for influence as he
possessed is not acquired in a day, and just when its
worth was being proved he was taken from us.
Surely these gifts and graces are not now as if they
had never been, or as if, once granted, they had been
idly wasted! Can that earnest, patient cultivation
really have been gratuitous, and the unselfish instinct
that inspired it mistaken? Were it so, the whole
universe looks out of joint. The more I consider
such lives as that of your brother—lives, I mean,
which, bearing promise of so rich a harvest, are yet
cut off before the full harvest can possibly have been
realised—the more my conviction grows that the
passing of such men as he is not death, but only " the
birth which we call death." '

II.

THE following is an extract from a letter written to
his brother Edward from St. Leonards :—

'Life has passed rapidly amid the genial surroundings of St. Leonards. Certainly I like the seaside.
Even being at school by the sea has not taken away
my liking for it. To-day we have had a fairly good
sea—roughish waves, a somewhat deep green colour,
a few black-sailed barks, no sun, a number of clouds,
a general seaside smell. One is more or less reminded
of New Brighton! Was one ever happier than when
one played at Egremont by the sea or walked towards

Wallasey? Shall we ever live over again our child-life? Is it, can it be gone for ever? Is there not still another child-life for us, coming from Him from whom all youth comes? Eternity is ever young. The Eternal is the source of all youth. Perhaps once again on the "shores of Eternity" we shall play together, men and yet children, old but still young, perhaps we shall once more find joy, simple joy in the very simple, in what seems to others the commonplace. Perhaps some day our imagination will be able to make towers of sand into something more than sand, into what we used to make them when we two played together, and lodged with George at Liscard. Meanwhile, I am your brother, Forbes.'

III.

THE following are extracts from a letter written to T. H. M. (on April 11, 1891), to whom several other letters in this volume were addressed It was written soon after Forbes Robinson had been reading Professor Maurice's Lectures on the Apocalypse, and embodies many of the thoughts contained in these Lectures.

'We have to choose, all of us, always, between the worship of the Lamb and the worship of the Beast, whose deadly world worship S. John the Divine or the Theologian, as the Church calls him, has shown in this same book—between living a

life of absolute self-sacrifice, such as is the life
of the Godhead, and worshipping and living the
life of the Beast. When we love Majesty, Beauty,
Intellect, Usefulness (the Lion, the Man, the Eagle,
the Calf) apart from God, when we do not recognise
that all come from God, that it is the Christ in man
or woman which is alone worth anything, we worship
the Beast : God guard us always from it. It is
our privilege to follow the Lamb whithersoever He
goeth, and we read where He went on earth and
where He goes now in the Bible. Humanity is even
now married to Christ, married to utter self-sacrifice,
the Lamb (xix. 7) ; the Church, the Beloved City
(xx. 9) does represent humanity. We are in the
millennium; departed saints are ruling (xx. 3). They
rule for a long period of time, "a thousand years."
Though Satan does and will break in upon that
rule with his miserable "tyranny of darkness," yet
departed saints are ruling. They have part in the
" first resurrection "—they rise directly they " sleep,"
when men say " they die "—the wicked have a death
of the soul, a " second death," being selfish, they
were dead here, they are dead there at present.
When good men die, they live again in Christ—
body, mind and soul die to live again. The saints
are ruling. Pray not to them, but for them. They
are one with us. They are helping us. They, like
us, still need God's help and love. Though Satan is
ever coming up against the loved city (xx. 9), he
shall finally be, nay potentially is, defeated, for the
decisive battle of the campaign was fought by the
Lamb on Calvary. Let us remember, all of us who

have been baptised into God's name, that we belong to a city, and that it is our own fault if we do not recognise that we are "kings and priests." Read on and you will see how always there is a "great white throne" of purity and judgment, how all who die are judged—how those who do wrong are cast into a fire of torment, an eternal fire, for the fire is no temporal thing, it has nothing to do with time. Call it what you will, conscience, remorse, misery, we fall into a "fire" when we do wrong. Thank God that we do! Thank Him that there is a lake of fire, that utter love does not forsake us, and will not let us alone, but burns us with the fire of love, until we come to our Father. There is, thank God, a "wrath of the Lamb"—a wrath of love, which will not leave us till we turn to Love, and love. Then look at the 21st chapter, "The sea is no more." We are one in Christ Jesus. We can hold fellowship (κοινωνίαν) one with another, when time and space divide us; all we are one, those who are dead, those who are living, those who are near each other, those who are absent: we are all one, there is no sea to divide us, no restless sea to separate us: Love jumps over all limits. We are all one man in Christ Jesus. Yes, the "holy city" does come from Heaven, and is in our midst; all who are in His Church are members of that city: we have such a position. You and I believe that we belong to one of the purest branches of that Church, of that Humanity which is redeemed and married to Christ; let us live as if we did, and pray for those who see less light, and yet are one with us in Christ Jesus. God's Tent is with men:

God does wipe away our tears (xxi. 4) as S. John
said He would. He comes to us and teaches us the
meaning of pain, and we feel His hand wiping our
eyes. Death is no more, as S. John said it would be
no more. We are one with those who are gone :
they are watching, ruling, loving, praying for us. Let
us live worthy of them, and watch and pray for and
with them. Do we fear for God's Church, and want
to exclude people whom we think wicked ? Let us
be careful how we do it. God has said that nothing
bad can enter that city. We are married to the
Lamb (9). Let us live as though we were. We
must be either members of God's city, and be
married to Christ, or members of Babylon, the
world's city, and be of a harlot. If you would see
the end of the Harlot, read chap. xvii. Are we
groping in darkness ? God is our Luminary. Do
we fear for the Kingdom ? It has a "wall great and
high ": we need not fear. Do we wish to narrow it
in order to suit our own narrow views ? We cannot
do so, for at every point of the compass there are a
perfect number of gates, and new members are ever
entering and recognising their position. Do we fear
that we are not connected with the past, nor one
with those who have gone before ? The wall of the
city (14) has twelve foundations, and on them the
names of the Apostles. Are we wanting to measure
it ? God has done so, we cannot (16). The size is
perfect, and we know that it is measured by a truly
human because a truly divine standard (17). Everything reflects God—everything is like pure glass (18).
If we separate the Church from God, all is gone.

He is the Light (there is a "Son of Man" ever walking among the candlesticks). Do we fear that all will be reduced to dull uniformity when all are perfect? God knows better: "Every kind of precious stone" adorns the city's walls (19). With emphatic repetition S. John tells us how each pure and beautiful excellency in man's character has a place in the city (19, 20). When shall we really learn that these are the only jewels of worth? Everything of worth in the world is there, everything pure and everything good, for the streets are of "pure gold," and the foundations are all most precious stones. Nothing is perfect in itself, all is perfect as it reflects God ; the street, though of pure gold, shows the light through by its transparency (διαυγής). . . . Let us remember that there is no temple there (22). The moment we set up anything or any person and worship them instead of the Christ, we become worshippers of the Beast instead of the Lamb. Do not let us set up Priests and Ritual and worship them, let us only worship the Christ as He shines through them, as He is reflected in them, as we can recognise His Beauty and Grace in them. All our mistakes arise from not making Him the Centre of all. How I long to feel this more myself. You know that I don't mean this controversially. I recognise the use of ritual and a little of the glory of the priesthood. God begins with one person, one thing, one day, one place, and He shows us the sacredness of these, not as if they were intrinsically more sacred than others, but that we may learn by regarding one building and house as holy, that all buildings and houses are holy ; that we may learn by loving one person well, to love all mankind as we love that person ; that we may learn by keeping one day, Sunday, holy, that all days are holy ; that we may learn by partaking of one common sacred food, that all food is sacred ; that we may learn by reverencing one man and place, to reverence all men and places ; that we may learn by contemplating the privileges of God's ministers that this is a pledge and assurance of our privileges also, and by using our privileges as Churchmen, that this is a pledge of what is in store for all mankind ; that we may learn that all life is a sacrament, and that God is all, and in all. We have learnt to love one or two very dearly, we have learnt to regard as sacred everything of theirs, their letters, aye, and the commonest things they use ; God has taught us in this way that He Who loves us all (so much that His Son became man and lived and died and lives for man) must regard as sacred everything we use, everything. God teaches us in this way that we must love others, as we do love a few, we must extend and deepen our love for the few and include others also, and we shall find our love for the nearest and dearest deepen. "Little Children," said the "Theologian," "let us love one another" Let us treat all men as we treat those whom we love best. For those we love best we would do anything that we could. God loved us so intensely that He has done and is doing everything He can for us. For those we love best we would die : we would be pleased to be their servants, their menials, their

slaves. God's Son did die for us: He became a
" slave ": " He took upon Him the form of a slave."
God loves us intensely—loves us better than we
love our very dearest friend. It is because He loves
us so that He can be and is angry. It is because
Christ is a Lamb that He can be angry. Think of
what that means, " the wrath of the Lamb." Aye,
and if we love like men, nobly, purely, divinely, we
too must be angry at every fault which tends to
make our loved ones selfish, and so bestial and
devilish, for every sin makes a man bestial and
devilish. If we love a person well, we will live a
pure life for his sake. Christ did that for us. " For
their sakes I purify myself." We find it comparatively easy to love a few well, but hard to love
all. Christ loves all, even those with whom we have
least sympathy, intensely. And we do not love
purely and divinely anyone at all, unless we are
willing for their sakes to live a pure and divine life.
When we love, we are truly united to and in God,
for " God is love." This is, this must be, the centre
of all true theology. It was the supreme doctrine
of S. John, the " Theologian." Read on, and you
will see that no human or " natural " light of sun
and moon lights our city (23). The Lamp is the
Lamb. The nations shall walk by and through
its light—the nations—national distinctions are not
lost sight of in that city : the nations are there,
England, France, Germany, Italy, all nations, for
the nation is sacred. God " seals " the nations for a
special work, and seals each division, each county,
each " tribe " for their own work. (*Cf.* Chap. **vii**, 5-8.)

He has set them apart, and though national convulsions come, yet the Son of Man is ever appearing in those convulsions, and the nations are sealed :
they were "sealed" in the Apocalypse before the
accounts of the fall of God's earthly city of Jerusalem
and man's earthly city, Babylon. Let us pray for
our nation and our Queen and her Ministers and all
those who rule us, pray for any we know or have
heard of by name, and the rest generally, and we
shall find our interest in the affairs of the nation
grow, we shall feel that we are Englishmen, and that
England has a work in God's universe peculiarly her
own. Yes, and the kings of the earth bring their
glory into the city (34). There are ranks still
recognised in God's city, though we are all slaves
of Christ—love has enslaved us. The gates are
never shut ; those who are within are all pure and
have their names written in the "Book of Life":
they are truly living. All baptized men and women
and children who are living here or living now in
Heaven, are members of God's city. God will take
care that the city is kept pure and that the self-
seeking shall not enter. It is possible, as our Lord
clearly says, that men who have never had our
privileges and never been baptized, shall enter the
Kingdom and the sons of it be cast into the darkness
" outside " of the city of Light. Read the 22nd
chapter and you will see that S. John was shown
the river coming from God the Father and the Son,
—the River of Life,—the Spirit that quickeneth.
That is our drink, and our food is described further
on, the Tree of Life, which Adam could not get at,

but which we have. No wonder that S. John says we thirst no more and hunger no more. For S. John himself tells us that our Master Jesus Christ said that all who eat His flesh and drink the water He provided would hunger and thirst no more. Interpret S. John here by his own words elsewhere, or rather the words of Christ that he has recorded, "Behold I come quickly." Christ is ever coming. Every judgment is the Son of Man coming, coming with clouds, it is the wrath of the Lamb; Christ did come at the fall of Jerusalem, as He said He would. (*Cf.* S. Matt. xxiv., and esp. v. 34.)

'S. John himself says that the anti-Christ is he who denies that Christ is ever coming in the flesh, 2 S. John, 7. Are we ever anti-Christ? Christ is ever coming to us: each time we see a generous deed and hear a man speak nobly and bravely and purely, and see a beautiful sight in nature, the Christ comes to us, for "all things were made in Him," and every life worth anything is the Christ-life. Wherever we find out anything in science, literature, history, art, theology, nature, we find Christ, for He is "the Truth." Wherever we see true life in man or beast or animal, we see Christ, for He is "the Life." Wherever we see anything pointing us to our kind and holy Father, Who is blessed for ever and ever, we see the Christ, for He is "the Way" to God: "I am the Way, the Truth and the Life." His life around, within, us is our "Light" as S. John tells us. He is, and ever was, in the world, but the world never recognised Him, and never does. He comes and came all through the world's history

(S. John, i. 11) to His own home, and its inmates
always are refusing His entrance. (The words in
S. John i. 1-13 describe the world before and after
the Incarnation, the Incarnation is described in v. 14.)
The final condemnation of the wicked is not that
they do not belong to "church" or "chapel" but that
they have refused to recognise the Christ in man,
the Christ coming in the flesh: " Ye have not done
it to the least of these," and therefore, *ipso facto*, "ye
have not done it to Me." Every man has the Christ
in him ; Christ comes to us in every child and tells
us how He loves us and how simple we must be.
. . . Let us thank God that perfect Purity and
perfect Power are seated on the pure "white throne";
thank God that we are man, that we are all one, and
pray that we all may recognise the position, and live
as one with saints on earth and saints in Heaven,
and saints yet to come.'

INDEX

Printed in England at THE BALLANTYNE PRESS
SPOTTISWOODE, BALLANTYNE & CO. LTD.
Colchester, London & Eton